Minetta Lane

A. Robert Allen

ISBN: 978-0-578-58057-9

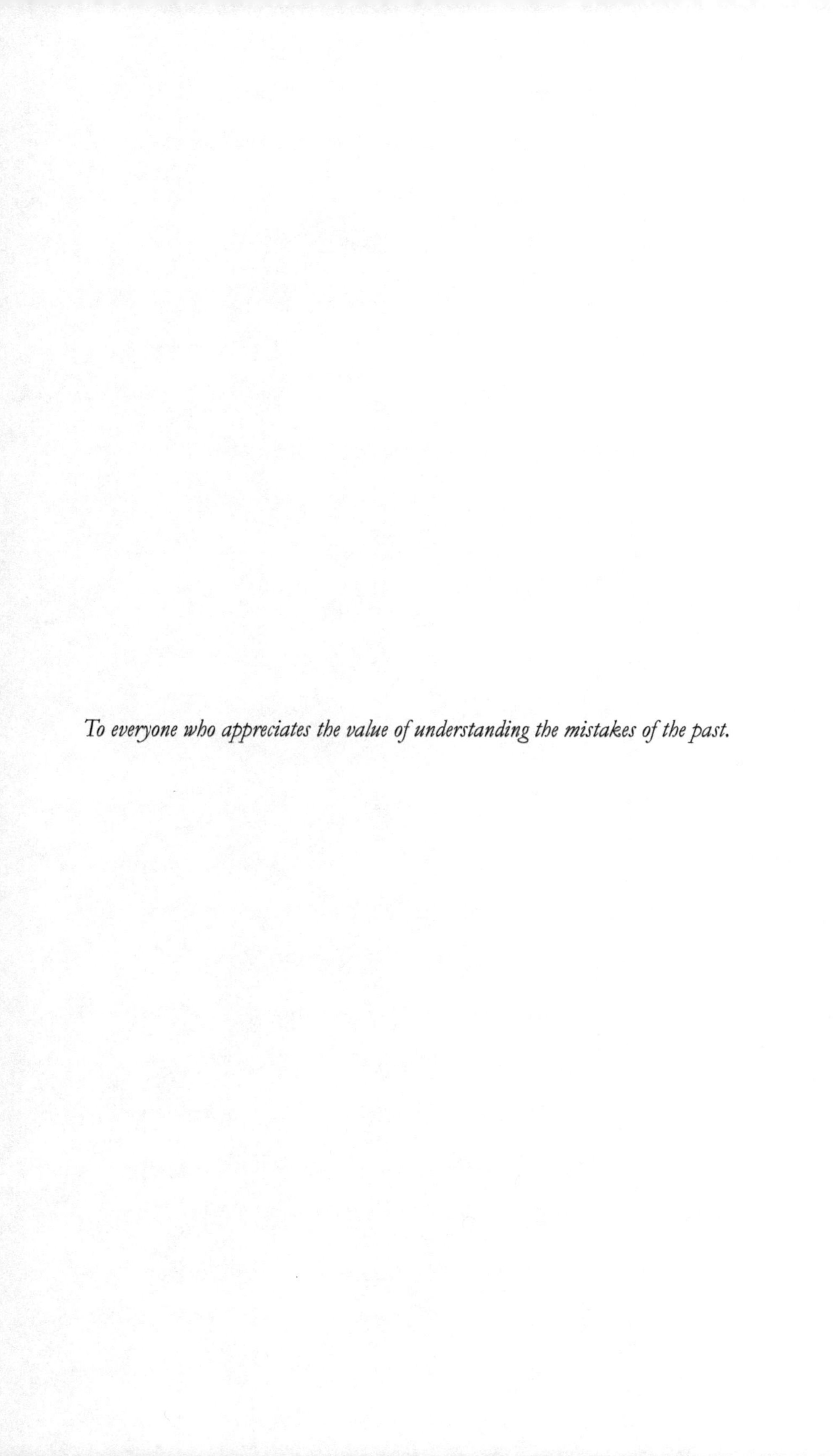

To everyone who appreciates the value of understanding the mistakes of the past.

Part One

*New York,
June 5–12
1904*

CHAPTER 1

The Minettas

BLACK WAS WHITE and White was Black in the Minettas, where both the roads and the rules curved in unusual directions. The point at which Minetta Lane intersected with Minetta Street was the heart of a neighborhood that adhered to a race-based code. The street followed the crooked path of an old covered-up creek, giving the area yet another nickname: The Bend. Everyone was well advised to proceed with caution on either of the Minettas, but Black residents had a permanent pass. Whites became immediate targets, except for the Irish gangsters, who walked the streets with impunity because even the thugs in the Bend gave respect when respect was due.

"Got 'em when he came 'round the corner. Couldn't believe all the money he had on him," Nine-Finger Nate bragged as he gripped a stack of bills with his left hand, which did not feature an index finger, while celebrating his success with his right. "He needed me to 'splain why the cash mine, so I clubbed him 'til he understood. Not enough to bring any police down here . . ."

The leader of the group, who went by the name Blood, reassured his men. "No cops gonna come down here—ain't been here for years. Remember the copper who chased Nine-Finger on the avenue last week? He stopped dead in his tracks as soon as we all waved hello. The police know better than to come in here." Blood paused when he spotted an inebriated White man wobbling in the distance.

Nine-Fingers stated the obvious. "Has no idea where he is. Drunk as shit. Who next?"

Blade raised his hand and the whispers began. "Right this way. We got something for ya. Yep, keep on coming."

They all muffled their laughter as the man, in his twenties, stumbled toward them. Blade disappeared into a tenement, kneeled behind a trapdoor, and pulled the intoxicated man into the basement, relieving him of both his money and his boots. The man was rewarded for his cooperation with a little cross, carved surface-level on his leg with a knife—Blade's signature move. Those who fought were branded in a more conspicuous manner. Blade's efforts didn't yield much of a payday, but the men approved of his new footwear.

Blood interrupted the congratulations with a clap of his hands. A Black man stood at the entrance to the lane and appeared to be about the same age as their last visitor. The rules were clear—if he lived in the area, they'd let him proceed unmolested. Otherwise, Black or White didn't matter.

"Man, if that boy turned to his side, you couldn't see him at all. He may be long, but he sure ain't wide! Won't be much trouble at all. Hope we don't know him," Nine-Finger said.

⊷═◉ ◉═⊶

Bodee Rivers rested against a lamppost at the Sixth Avenue end of the lane. Despite the dim lighting, which provided a better view of shadows than people, he had observed the drunken White man walk down the road and disappear into a building. He checked the piece of paper in his hand one last time. *Yup, 17 Minetta Lane. What should I do? Don't have any money or other place to go, but there's no way I'm getting through those guys.* He glanced to the left and right for alternatives, but found none so he remained frozen in place. *Need to go back. Can't get through.*

The men moved into the street as they greeted an elderly woman with nods of deference. The woman exchanged some words with the group, pointed, and the entire contingent began a slow march toward Bodee's position.

Are they coming for me or are they going somewhere past me? he thought. *Better hide and be ready to run. I'll try another time.*

The group advanced to a spot about twenty feet away from the end of the block and the woman held up her right hand. "Stop. It's him." Meanwhile, Bodee ran into a nearby alley on Sixth Avenue, slipped behind a tall crate, and stood still with his back flush to the wall. *Never find me here—no way, but what if they do?*

Ain't no way out. How do I keep getting myself in these situations? Made a mistake coming here.

The woman continued alone, but hesitated after turning right onto Sixth and peered down the street. A cat jumped from its perch above the crate, startling Bodee, who took a quick step out and another back into his hiding place. He dug back into the wall, hoping he hadn't been discovered.

The woman walked toward the source of the sound and stopped when she spotted the tip of a shoe sticking out from behind the box—she waited. After a few moments of awkward silence, she called out, "A grown man shouldn't be hiding like a scared boy. Come on out." He didn't move.

"No one will hurt you and nobody here with me. I got something to show you." She removed a tattered photograph from her bag. "Bodee, I'm your Grandma Juba. Spent time with you when you nothing more than a baby. This an old picture of your mama. Been expecting you. Walk by my side and as long as you with me, nobody will do you no harm. Welcome home."

Chapter 2

Madame Juba

Bodee entered the tenement expecting to find one of many tight living spaces, but instead found a spacious parlor featuring a small round table with two chairs in the center of the room. A shelf, positioned next to the front door, contained a single unlit candle. Images of Christian saints adorned the walls, and a long bench, containing a variety of items, occupied one of the back corners. He paused to examine the back bench before following his grandmother up the stairs. *What are these figurines and these bottles . . . what's inside? What's that smell coming from the jar?* She called down from the second floor, "You don't understand what you're touching, so put the jar down and come upstairs."

Juba pointed. "This where you slept—right on the cot in the corner. Your mother, Akua, grew up in this apartment and you started out here twenty years ago."

Bodee struggled to decide which question to ask first, and began with the obvious, "Why did you think I would be coming tonight and how did you recognize me?"

Juba paused, took a seat, and her severe features contorted. She swallowed hard before answering. "Didn't say anything about tonight, only knew you'd be here when the sun going down. Been walkin' out every night looking for you for the last few days."

Bodee resisted the temptation to ask the logical follow-up question: why at sundown? Juba's stare morphed into a glare. *This woman may be my grandmother, but she's a stranger and has all of these criminals in the neighborhood afraid of her,* he thought. *She doesn't have any interest in giving me information, but where else can I go? Let me be quiet.* He settled back in his chair, slumped his shoulders, and stared out the window.

"You give up this fast? After all these years, you stop asking questions after I make a face? You nothing but a little boy who better become a man real soon, or you won't survive in the Bend."

"I'm a twenty-year-old grown man and you might understand me more if you ever paid me a visit."

Juba sprang out of her seat and slapped her grandson square in the face. *Whap!* He placed his hand over his right cheek and shifted in his chair with his eyes focused on the table.

Juba sighed as she reached for his hands. "You don't ever talk to me like that! Do you understand?"

"Yes . . . yes, ma'am."

"Guess I got some explaining to do—been a long time, but I tell you what I tell you, and not all at once. Tonight we talk about one big thing. Sound all right to you?"

"Sounds fine." Bodee sat back and waited for his absentee grandmother to explain herself.

"The big thing I teach you tonight is about your people, the Ashanti. My grandfather grew up in Africa. Slavers took him about a hundred and twenty years ago to what is now Haiti. He died when my father was small. The master moved with my father and all the house slaves to New Orleans."

"My daddy a slave his whole life, but he a houngan, which is a priest. Needed to learn in secret though, because the master couldn't find out. I born in New Orleans in 1840, and discovered my family history from my father and I told your mother everything. What she tell you?"

"She said you escaped slavery and traveled up north toward the end of the war, but nothing about anything down South."

"So much more to tell. Hold on to who you are—can't ever lose that. You understand?"

"Yes, Grandma Juba. I do."

"Just call me Juba."

"All right."

"My father like me and you. Better I tell you about this anyhow."

What does she mean? Bodee thought. *I'm like her and her father; she doesn't understand what I'm like at all.* He decided to let her finish her story. "Please tell me."

"My father smart and could do special things."

"What kinds of things?"

"Your mother didn't tell you nothin'. You and my father the same, so you needed his name, Bodua. Means either leader or protector in Ashanti. Daddy always a leader, and you'll be a protector. Bodua is your real name—it got switched up to Bodee."

"It's only a name and I don't feel like I can protect people." Bodee glanced in the mirror across from the table at the image of his rail-thin frame and its lack of any noticeable musculature. My whole life, I've been . . ." He stopped himself.

"What you trying to say?"

"Nothing, go on. What about your name?"

"Juba mean born on Monday. All important things happen on Monday." Juba chuckled. "Like I said, your granddaddy a houngan and some people around here think I'm a mamba—a female priest—but it not true. So this the big thing I promised to tell you. You with me, so far?"

"Yes, ma'am."

"Even though I'm not a mamba, I let them think what they want when they ask for help downstairs. Sometimes what I say works, other times not so much, so I'm careful when not sure. Hard to explain. Someone comin' in a few minutes."

"Is this what you do in the parlor? People come to ask for advice?"

"I keep havin' to tell you . . . nothing's that simple, but you'll understand after you listen. He'll be here soon. Sit right here."

Juba walked down the stairs and lit the candle on the center table. She heard a knock on the door.

"Come in."

"Need your help. Got a problem with Martha." The hulking man eased into his seat, making sure it could handle his weight, and took out his handkerchief to wipe the tears streaming from his eyes. "She left me, and I got two young kids. Can't go on without her. What I gonna do?"

Juba put her hand over his and started to make a deep guttural moan, "Hmm . . . hmmm." She released her guest's hands, opened her eyes, and closed them again. The moaning resumed and continued until her eyes opened for a second time. She studied every inch of the man's face and said, "Sorry to tell you, but your Martha dead, and the kids do need someone to take care of them. Can't waste time—many women happy to be with you. Start a new family. You miss her, but she dead. Not sure how, so don't ask, but she dead. Find a new woman."

Juba bid the man farewell, headed upstairs, and sat across from her grandson. "So what you think?"

Bodee took some time to respond. "Not sure what to think. Are you for real or playing games?"

"Fair question. Answer is . . . I'm not always for real, but I never play games."

"What do you mean?"

"His wife sleeps 'round with almost every man in the Bend—she's a whore and he's a fool. She ran away last week and no one thinks she's coming back. Remember what I said, 'she dead,' which is the right thing—he got to think like she dead and start with someone new. No Voudou, no black magic, nothing but common sense."

"Tell me about when you're being real. What is *real* like?"

"Not ready to tell until you ready to tell and I already said too much for now. You use your bed. Sleep well." Juba excused herself and went to her bedroom, leaving Bodee alone with his thoughts. He felt comfortable lying in the bed of his infancy. Despite the unfamiliar surroundings, he realized he was, in fact, home.

Chapter 3

Don't Go There

BODEE WOKE TO the aroma of bacon and expected to find his mother standing by the stove across from where he slept in their home in Brooklyn. The reality of his situation set in, however, as his grandma prepared his plate—eggs in front, bacon around the edges, and a small piece of bread in the middle. *Just like Mama!*

"Don't be so surprised," Juba said. "Who do you think taught your mother how to cook?"

He pulled on his clothes and sat by the table. "Thanks for breakfast. I want to eat and head out—need to find work."

"Fine. You should find a job, but I don't need money. Take your time to find the best one you can. Not planning to charge any grandson of mine no rent."

Bodee nodded and his smile gave away his tremendous sense of relief. "Thanks. The food looks delicious." He cleaned his plate with four strokes of his fork.

"You ate those eggs like you got a decent appetite. Why you so scrawny?"

"Not sure. Started to eat a lot when I began playing baseball. I was real fast but didn't hit with power." Bodee held up his puny arms and flexed.

"Nothing to make a joke about—being weak won't help you in this world and pointing it out with jokes don't make it any better."

"Yeah, you're right, but I can't gain any weight. Almost got on a professional baseball team, though, the Brooklyn Monitors."

"What happened?"

"It don't matter, you got any more grub?"

"Sure do, give me a few minutes."

Bodee caught a glimpse of his baseball shoes and glove, which were peeking out of the top of his bag, and thought back to his tryouts with the Monitors. *It was nice they let me play in that last practice game, but I knew I couldn't play with those guys. No matter now.*

⊷▬ ⬤▬⊷

Bodee shuffled side to side in the batter's box and scanned the field—both the first and third basemen were inching toward him. *The pitcher is slow on his feet, so I'll bunt straight ahead this time.* The ball came straight down the middle. *Perfect!* He extended his bat and placed the bunt directly toward the pitcher, who scrambled forward and scooped up the slow dribbler, but rushed his throw. The ball sailed over the head of the first baseman and Bodee safely continued on to second base.

The pitcher turned to Bodee. "Why don't you swing the bat like a man! You bunt every damn time. We all know you gonna do it. That ain't all there is in baseball."

The second baseman walked over. "Don't worry about him, he'll be happy enough when the season starts and you make the pitchers on the other teams nervous. Where'd you learn to run like that? You as fast as the wind!"

"Just doing my best. Speed is my thing. Wish I could hit a little better."

Bodee took a long lead off second base. The pitcher grimaced, stepped off the mound, and called out to the manager, "Listen, boss, I'm just trying to get into shape. I don't need this skinny kid torturing me while I do it."

The manager answered, "Stop your belly-aching. This is good practice for you." He looked at Bodee and smiled.

The pitcher scowled at the manager and then at Bodee. He kicked the dirt and tried to settle down as he began his windup, but he was unsuccessful. The pitch went into the ground and got away from the catcher. Bodee slid into third base.

The manager clapped his hands and stopped the practice for the day. "I've seen enough. All you players wait on the other side of the field." He motioned to Bodee. "Come with me, we got to talk."

"We have one open spot and it's between you and Williams. You run as fast as anyone I ever seen, but you don't hit for shit. I need a little more power from you. They play you so far in because of the bunting. If you could hit a little bit, they'd need to back up, which would make your bunting even better. You understand?"

"Well, yes, sir, but I never been able to hit so much. I try to connect and hit ground balls because I can beat out the throw."

"Everyone knows that—you do it every damn time. Once you start hitting the ball into the outfield, you'll stretch singles into doubles and that's when you'll really be valuable to us."

"Does this mean I'm not valuable now, so I don't get the last spot?"

"It's either you or Williams, like I said. He's a slugger, but he's getting old and doesn't have your speed."

Bodee looked over at his competition. "I remember Williams from when I was a kid coming to see you guys play. I couldn't ever hit like him. I understand."

"What the hell is wrong with you, kid? I'm telling you who you going up against and what his weaknesses are, and you're ready to give up on the last spot? You ain't got no fight in you?"

"Don't know about all that, but I can't hit for power like Williams."

"Right now, you're all speed and no power, but until you get some fight in you, that will never change. Come back next year, kid, when you got your head right." The manager shook Bodee's hand and then screamed, "Williams, get over here."

⊷▭ ▭⊷

Bodee noticed a small wooden base on the kitchen table with two indentations, one in the shape of a triangle and the other a hexagon, just as Juba finished up at the stove. The wood was a dark brown and the grain was highlighted with layers of stain. He reached into his pocket and pulled out his mama's unusual necklace—a tube with a short string passing through one of the many small holes at the top. The grain of the wood matched, and it fit on one side—a pepper shaker.

Juba put down his plate and smiled. She reached for the necklace buried under her nightgown and placed her cylinder into the triangular slot on the left. "Yes, that's right, salt and pepper shakers."

"Mama said this gave her luck. She used to clutch it in her hands, almost like she praying. Always carried it with her."

Juba started to cry and took some time to gather herself. "My baby girl still loved me after all of these years and problems." A broad smile emerged from the tears. "One day Akua had trouble at school when she little and I told her these shakers were magical and whenever she held it in her fist, I would be right there with her to help her and make her strong."

"The shaker was in her hand when she died."

Juba's tears were now in a free fall. "You and I lost so much time. Hold on to the pepper, and I'll be your salt, just like I was for Akua. Let's put these plates away and take a walk around the Bend. You need to understand what's safe and dangerous and we want everyone in the neighborhood to know you attached to me, because this, more than any pepper shaker, will keep you out of trouble."

⊷►▬◉ ◉▬◄⊷

The hustle and bustle of the evening retreated to a slow crawl in the morning. The criminal element slept in most days because their *work* took place late at night.

"Bodee, these houses along here are all whorehouses. Some are connected to the bars, like the one across the street—a place called Tigress. No sign out front, but that the name, trust me. Next door is a mixed bar called, Snake Eyes, where our local Black folk drink with the Irish gangsters, and the whores from Tigress work the club for customers. Nothing for a twenty-year-old boy. Understand?"

"Yes, ma'am."

"Remember, being family to me will protect you if you do the right thing and go about your business, but if you start going into those places, you're on your own. One more thing—the place at the end of the block is called Slide— also not for you. Slide is a bar for men who like men—do you get what I mean?"

"Yeah. Stay away."

"We got two places comin' up, the signs say 'Restaurant,' and 'Barbershop.' The restaurant ain't got no stove and the barbershop ain't got no scissors. Those places do a different kind of business that—"

Bodee interrupted, "That I should stay away from."

"Smart boy. You catching on!"

"I'm not sure any place is okay for me around here."

"Not true. You can go where we live and the general store on the corner. I don't—"

Bodee interrupted his grandmother's thought as he jerked her away from the front of the "Barbershop" sign. At first, Bodee's abrupt action confused her, but after she took hold of his hands, she smiled. A moment later, a bucket of dirty water tossed from a third-floor window landed on the exact spot she stood before being pulled away.

A woman poked her head out of the window and called down to the street, "Madame Juba, I'm so sorry. Nothing but my fool of a boy. Apologies."

⊷▨▩ ▩▨⊷

Juba waited until they both climbed the back stairs to begin the conversation that was long overdue. "Either you start or I will. One way or the other, makes no difference to me."

"What you mean?"

"You know what I mean. Why you pull me back the way you did by the barbershop?"

"Not sure. Just did it."

"That's all you got to say?"

Bodee pulled at his shirt to loosen the collar. Sweat poured down his brow and he scanned the room for help as if some object in the apartment would give him a question to ask or a new direction to take the conversation. Nothing helped, but she took pity on him. "You're not ready. Remember what I said yesterday—I'll only tell when you tell, and I'm not changing my mind. Go out and look for your job—we need a break anyway."

He dashed down the stairs and out to the street. Finally, he could breathe.

CHAPTER 4

Job Hunting

ARMED WITH HIS high school diploma and the help-wanted section of the news-paper, Bodee started looking for a job. His goal: to become a full-time clerk in an office. Some hiring managers told him there were no positions available despite the job listing in the paper and the other applicants waiting to be seen. Others were more direct and explained that Colored folks had no place in an office. A few actually spoke to him, but determined he lacked the basic qualifications. After no success throughout the morning, it was clear he needed a new strategy.

A pamphlet with a headline that read "Cool off at Pier 6" blew by Bodee as he bent to tie his shoelace. He chased it down and carefully read the advertise-ment, which described the new floating baths the city had set up to help people battle the heat. Bodee remembered the hours he spent at the beach in Brooklyn and all of the compliments he received from his high school classmates about his strong swimming abilities. He headed over to Pier 6.

⋆⇒═◉ ◉═⇐⋆

"Need a job, sir. Who can I talk to?"

"Listen, boy, don't want no more deckhands or anyone else for the grunt work. You're out of luck."

"No, sir. I'm looking for work in the baths." Bodee pointed to a Help Wanted sign on the wall behind the man's head and said, "I want to apply for the life-guard job because I swim real well. They say I'm a *natural*."

The man laughed under his breath. "Hold your thought and wait right here. I'll be right back."

Bodee scanned the setup of the baths. The structure was supported by eight pontoons, four on each side. He read the signs—two separate swimming areas about ninety-five feet long and sixty feet wide would serve adults and children. The adult pool was four and a half feet deep and the children's pool only two and a half feet. Despite the shallow waters, lifeguards were needed. Bodee's high school classmates were not unusual—very few people in the city could swim. The diving board brought on an image of children jumping into the water with smiles on their faces. Bodee didn't hear the men approaching.

"Wake up, boy. Tell my friends what you told me."

"I want to apply for a job as a lifeguard."

"No, you said something different before. I thought you said you are a *natural* swimmer. Right?"

"Well, yeah. The teachers at my school told me I'm a *natural.*"

The man repeated Bodee's statement with a high-pitched voice while prancing on his toes. "The teachers say I'm a natural!" His two colleagues laughed and Bodee tried to leave but one of the men grabbed him by the collar. "Not so soon. Need to school you a bit." The man turned to his coworkers. "I think he got this all wrong. What do we think he's a natural at?"

"Picking up shit!"

"No, taking shit!"

"Yeah, he's a shit natural, or no, a natural shit! Yeah, that's what he is! I guess it works both ways!"

After two more minutes of finger-pointing, back-slapping, and general hysteria, one of the men put his hand up and the other two quieted down. "Thanks for the laugh, you stupid Darkey. Do you think anyone wants your Black ass in this pool? We'd need to drain it after each time you went in—the fancy word is called contamination. That's what you are, boy, pure and simple. No decent White folk gonna want to go into any water you touched." A goodbye kick in the butt marked the end of Bodee's potential career as a lifeguard. The walk back home to Minetta Lane gave him a chance to reconsider his job objective, as the single dollar bill in his pocket desperately needed some company. *I'll take anything at all—full-time, part-time, permanent, or temporary. None of it matters. I just need money.*

Chapter 5

Triple N

"Pa, I don't need this much for one bottle of milk."

"Do as I say, Eddie. Be a good gossoon, take this money, and bring me what I asked for. Go on, off with ya."

Edward Murphy Senior had three things to do before his son returned: pack his bag, finish his last bottle of whiskey, and leave. He reasoned one last time with himself. *This is what the boy needs to become a man. Same thing happened to me. Sure, I was a little bigger, but my parents left me on my own too—the boy's got to be able to fend for himself. That's the way of the world. After all, he's got some money, this apartment for another week, and neighbors who'll help him out. All he's got to do is flash his thousand-dollar smile.* Senior wiped a tear from his face. *This isn't time to be soft. I'm doing this for him—he's better off without me.*

One more sip and he was gone.

Edward Junior came home from the store and waited for his father by the window. Often his dad stumbled home drunk and needed some help for the last few steps. After a week, the landlord moved him out to the street and Eddie sat on the curb. Eventually, the ten-year-old boy put on his father's shirt in an attempt to appear more mature, and went out into the city. Eddie needed to eat and sleep, but more than anything, he needed help.

He roamed the streets during the day and found different locations to take temporary shelter. Food was an issue until he discovered a restaurant manager partial to his glorious smile. At the end of his third day, Eddie discovered a nook behind a box in an alley where he slept undisturbed for three consecutive nights. On the fourth night in his special bedroom, he fell to the ground when someone moved the crate that bordered his space.

"Sorry, brother, didn't know this was your place. I guess you too late to get into the lodge, huh? Me too. Not so bad, though, kind of warm out tonight. Don't nobody take care of you?"

"Nah, my Da went away on a trip."

"Mine too, must be going around the world! Been gone four years! What paper you sellin'?"

"Paper?"

"Yeah, the only jobs for us are either being a newsie or a boot black. Don't see any black fingers . . . rather be a newsie any day. I work for the *Tribune* and I know the best spots. How about you?"

"I'm not sellin' anything."

"No problem. I'll help you out. My name is Two-Tooth Tommy. Can you guess why?" The older boy's mouth opened when he laughed and the obvious reason for his nickname became apparent.

"My name is Eddie."

"Your name ain't right for the business. Stand up."

Tommy glanced at tiny little Eddie Murphy, who swam in his father's over-sized button- down shirt. He took a minute and giggled, "Okay, we'll call you Triple N—stands for the No Neck Newsie! Shove over, I need some shut-eye before the morning."

⇥ ⇤

"Come on. Wake up. Today I'll show you how to be a newsie. Sleepin' is over. We need to head down to the Row," Tommy barked as Eddie got to his feet. "Follow me, don't say too much unless I tell you, and do what I do."

The two boys headed downtown to Newspaper Row, the home of most of the city's newspapers: *The World Telegram, The New York Sun, The Tribune, The Journal,* and *The Daily News,* among others.

"All the best dailies are here. A couple moved uptown because they want-ed the block named for them. Real fancy. *The Times* is on Forty-Second, so they call that Times Square. Why you think Thirty-Fourth Street is Herald Square?"

Eddie shrugged his shoulders.

"That's where *The Herald* moved! We're *Tribune* men—hope they don't move, don't want to be traveling to Tribune Square, wherever that'll be! Remember, do what I do."

⊷⊷⊷ ⊶⊶⊶

"You got any money, Triple N?"

"A little."

"Give the bucks over here."

Eddie reached into his pocket and pulled out his last four quarters.

"Okay, this will do. Today, you treat me, because I'm teachin' you." Tommy took two of the coins.

All of the boys crowded around the loading dock and Tommy walked forward with Eddie trailing behind. He called out to the man with the stacks. "I'll take two. One for me and one for him."

"Is he your guttersnipe, Tommy?"

"Yeah, he's with me."

"Seems a little too scrawny. You sure he can do this?"

Tommy raised his voice and turned to the other children. "I'm watching out for him. Anyone fucks with him, they fuck with me."

"Okay. Here you go." The man threw the papers to the boys. Eddie struggled with the king-size bundle.

"You need to toughen up to carry your stuff. We'll sell some close by, each one for a penny, so we double our money."

"Wow!"

"We're going to where the ferry docks. Best spot for us. Let me introduce you to some of the boys."

A few of the others gathered around. "Listen boys, this here Triple N, the No Neck Newsie!" They all erupted in laughter.

"Hey, I'm Slobering Sam."

"I'm Fat Franky."

"I'm Snot Snot."

They all nodded hello and scrambled to their corners. Within minutes, Triple N was crying out, "Read all about it."

Chapter 6

Snake Eyes

THE NEXT MORNING wasn't as welcoming as the last. Juba stood by the kitchen table, staring out the window at the brick wall of the neighboring building. She sighed, banged her mug against the tabletop, and headed back into her room. Bodee guessed she had second thoughts about giving him time to find work. She turned to him, grimaced, and returned to her room. *Better find something fast,* he thought.

Bodee left the apartment with no definite destination in mind. He recalled the warning about wandering around Minetta Lane, but felt comfortable in his new surroundings. The same gang of criminals who hid in the shadows during his first encounter with the neighborhood acknowledged his presence, or perhaps his connection with Juba, with a nod. He wondered why her supposed Voudou powers generated such tremendous respect.

Blood sipped his coffee by the stairs to Juba's tenement. "Word is you need to find work."

"Yeah, no luck yesterday."

"Something in an office doing paperwork, right?"

Bodee didn't understand the reason for Blood's sudden interest in his job search, but understood he and Juba were close. "Yeah, bookkeeping and general office work."

"Oh, so you're a numbers man. Might be something right here on the lane. Did you hear about a bar called Snake Eyes?"

"Yeah."

"They want to hire some kind of clerk. Opens up around noon. Ask for Silvy. Tell him I sent you."

"Thanks, Blood." Bodee appreciated the lead, but worried about both the source and the fact that his potential place of employment held a prominent spot on Juba's list of off-limits establishments.

⊷⊷◉ ◉⊶⊶

Bodee assumed most bars appeared better in the dim evening lighting. Snake Eyes, however, would require utter darkness to be presentable. The gaps in the ceiling, combined with several missing floorboards, created a certain inside/outside look. Given the early lunchtime hour, the only person present was a Black man with gray hair who stood behind the bar.

"Hey, you Silvy? Blood said you might need a bookkeeper."

"Yeah. How you know Blood?"

"He friends with my Grandma Juba."

"Blood ain't friends with nobody, son. Don't get confused, you better start wondering why he's so interested in you. Not his style. But I do need help with the books and ordering during the day before I open. You think you can handle those things?"

"Yes, sir."

"Stop this sir bullshit. You in the Bend, boy. Pick up the stack of bills on the table and tell me what you make of them."

Bodee glanced at the papers. "You got statements from your whiskey and beer supplier and they'll give you ten percent off if you pay by the first of the month. Also a note from a store sayin' if you don't settle up with them by the end of the day today, they'll come back for their table."

"Not bad. You think you can figure out ten percent off?"

"Yes, sir, I mean, Silvy."

"Next thing . . . I want you to take this here copy of the *Tribune* and tell me the headline and what the first story says."

Bodee spent the next five minutes explaining the major story featured in the paper. "How did I do? You thought I couldn't read?"

Silvy laughed. "No, boy, I'm the one who don't read so fast! Takes me all day to read the front page, so this will be our deal—you come in here every day around this time. Take care of the bills and explain the stories to me and I'll give you a few dollars. Don't want you in here after four—things change later in the day. Not the kind of place where you want to be. Deal?"

"Works for me."

"All right, you take this money over to the furniture store. The address is at the top of the paper. Bring the bill back to me tomorrow, marked paid. We'll have a problem if those folks come by later sayin' they want their table—you understand me?"

"I do. Thanks for the job."

Bodee started a long, slow walk across town to make the payment, holding the envelope with the cash along with his pepper shaker buried deep in his left front pocket. He passed a small cafe and noted the sign in the window, Juniors, and remembered one of his few trips as a child into the city with his mother.

"Son, listen to me. Today we in New York. This ain't Weeksville and you got to keep your eyes open and make sure you not gettin' yourself into no trouble. We're going to eat at a place with the best pie anywhere. I used to come here all the time. Next block over. The red sign says Juniors."

"I can't read yet."

"I know, tellin' you the name is all."

Four-year-old Bodee walked holding his mama's hand and spotted a woman on the other side of the street smiling and waving at him. His mother followed the direction of her son's return wave, became incensed, and scooped him up as she rushed across the street.

"How you know I'd be here? I done told you to leave me and my boy alone. You done enough damage."

The woman waved again at Bodee and blew him a kiss. Akua intervened. "You leave my boy be. You nothin' but a damn witch! How you know I'd be here? I asked you this question twice now, and I want an answer!"

"Didn't know you be here today. Just felt like soon and I knew it be 'round this time."

"You stay away from me and my boy. Stay away!"

Akua had lost her appetite and headed straight back to the ferry for the return trip to Brooklyn. After she calmed down, Bodee asked, "Who that woman who got you so mad?"

"My mother. They call her Juba, but she bad, through and through, and you got to stay away from her. You understand?"

"No. Why she bad?"

"Never you mind, Bodee—you too young to understand. Swear to me that if you ever see her again, you'll stay away."

"Swear?"

"Means you going to do what you say."

"Not going to swear then, Mama. That my grandma."

"Who do you think you talkin' to? You nothing but a little child and don't know what's best. Do what I say, Bodee. Remember, I'm your mama."

"Ain't Grandma Juba your mama?"

"I'm not going to tell you again. You keep coming back and coming back, but this over. Do what I say and stop all of this nonsense. The child don't tell the parent what to do."

"So why you tell your mama to stay away. She my Grandma Juba!"

Whack. Bodee received his first slap that day and then his second, when he asked his mother to swear she'd never do it again. The third and fourth came later that night and by the end of the week, Bodee stopped counting. He also stopped trying.

Bodee realized he'd been standing in front of Juniors the entire time he re-lived his childhood memory. The waitress came out and asked, "You okay? You lost or something?"

"I'm fine. Thanks for asking. I heard you got the best pie in New York and I can't decide between the apple or the blueberry."

"How about I give you a little of both? You look like you could put some meat on those bones."

"Sounds good to me!"

Bodee had his fill and thanked the waitress on his way out. He realized his mama was right about the pie, but wrong about a whole lot else.

Chapter 7

You Understand?

"Time for you to learn more about your family. You don't need to understand much more about people came before me, but I should tell you more about me and Akua. Fair enough?"

"Yes, but I don't have so much going back in time to tell you."

"Here's the thing. I'll go backward, but you got to tell me about things moving forward—sound like a plan?"

"Yes, ma'am."

"I'll go first after we start dinner. Help me set the table. Got some chicken and some potatoes."

"Sounds tasty!" Bodee walked toward the table and considered what he would say about *moving forward*, because Juba might be angry at the location of his new part-time job. *Maybe I'll start with something else.*

Grandmother and grandson ate in silence as they both decided how certain topics should be broached. The extra time to organize thoughts came to an end when Bodee took the last potato and eyed the final slice of chicken.

"You take the last piece of meat, and I'll start. Go ahead, now. Still don't know why you so skinny. Can't see how you could eat any more."

"It's your good cooking, Juba!" Bodee smiled as he bit into the last piece of chicken.

"Akua born in Orleans when I just twenty-three. Your grandfather a slave too, but he died before I gave birth to your mother. To this day, I don't understand what happened to him—too young to die the way he did, only forty years old. Found him dead one morning when I was six months pregnant. Same thing happened to Akua, but I wish I heard in time to be at the funeral—don't hold that against you 'cause you couldn't reach me, but I'm happy you got my letter and are here now."

"Me too, but I feel bad about not knowing how to reach you. The answer was always *no* whenever I asked to go visit you."

"How many times you ask her?"

Bodee paused and remembered the slaps and his eventual submission to his mother's will. "Not as many times as I should have."

"Least you being honest, but you should've pushed back some more. You don't seem to be so good at fighting back. I think this one of the things we'll work on. Sometimes, you shouldn't take no for an answer, but let's go back to the family. Your grandfather passed before Akua came into this world."

"Wow, so my mama never met her father, just like me."

"Don't mean nothing—lots of people never met their daddies, but things got bad after he gone. Master liked his work and if he lived I wouldn't have run. I wasn't of much use to Master after your granddaddy died and he told me he wanted to sell my baby soon as possible—said didn't need another Darkey baby—told me to my face, and said I should be happy I'd never be sold because *I'm* like family. Didn't even understand your mother was fixin' to be the biggest part of my family—needed to escape."

"Must've been hard being all the way down in New Orleans. You so far away from the North."

"Yeah, it was hard. I thought the river was the best way out, right up the Mississippi, but I needed to wait for the right ship. Found one when your mother only a few weeks old. The captain drank too much, and three slaves did most of the work on the boat. One of them took a chance on us. Me and Akua hid below for the whole time in a little room. Put towels all around to block the sound of her crying. Got up into Ohio and across to New York. Spent some time in your favorite place, Weeksville, at the Berean Baptist Church. Those people helped us and after a while I came into this place on Minetta Lane."

"Mama told me this part. She said most runaways kept goin' up to Canada. Why you stay?"

"Times bad in Manhattan back in 1863—riots right before we got here. The Irish fought the Blacks and the rich. They roughed up the wealthy, but hung lots of Colored folks, so many afraid for a spell. Not me, though. I did a favor for someone who owned this here house, and he let us stay. I been here ever since and your mama stayed until you almost one year old."

Juba paused and took a sip of water. "That all I got to say about goin' backward. What you got to tell me about goin' forward?"

"First, tell me how you figured which boat to take and why you thought you'd be safe in Manhattan?"

"Done told you . . . not gonna tell 'til you tell. Your turn."

Bodee paused for a minute to consider what level of detail he'd provide as he arranged the bones on his plate. "I searched for work in some offices in Manhattan, but I can't say many businesses were happy at the idea of working with a Colored man. Most managers didn't want to talk to me."

"So, no luck finding a job?"

"No luck."

"I'll ask you one more time, is there anything else you got to say going on with you, 'cause if there is and you don't tell me, we got a problem. You can stay here as long as you need to, but if we start having problems, you got to go somewhere else."

"Go somewhere else! Where? What do you mean?"

"Do you think anything will happen in this little neighborhood without Madame Juba knowin' 'bout it? Do you think you could take a job in the Bend without everyone tellin' me, without Silvy himself stopping by for permission? Everything runs through Blood and me."

"I thought you might be mad at me. You said not to go inside, so I planned to wait for the right time to tell you."

"Listen here, I told you not to go in that bar, but you did. Like if you a child and I told you not to go near the stove, but you did and got burned—you'd need to come for help right away because when something like that happens, there's no such thing as the right time. I'm tellin' you clear as day, you better be real careful in Snake Eyes—worst kind of people in this city drink in that saloon. Real easy to be burned in there even if you don't touch the stove, and if you do, you come to me right away. I keep askin' if you understand, and you keep sayin' you do, but this one thing you need to promise me. At the first sign of trouble, you come to me right away."

"For sure. This job is only until something else opens up."

"Interesting, that's the same I said twenty years ago when I moved to Minetta Lane. Time will tell."

Chapter 8

Lunch

"Your second day is going much better than the first, Triple N. Time for lunch. I eat with Slobbering Sam and a few of the other guys. We go down the block and check if the stores will give us any food and then we split everything up. You take the other side of the street and if you get to the alley by the warehouse before me, just tell them you're with Two-Tooth." Triple N nodded. The boys separated and worked their way through the neighborhood, which was home to a number of vegetable and fruit stands as well as a bakery and a butcher.

Some of the storekeepers chased Tommy out before he said a word. A few let him make his pitch before dismissing him. One confronted him as he entered. "You'll not steal from this store. You're nothing but a criminal."

"You don't know me. How can you say that? I work hard as a newsie."

"You're all criminals! That's why you're on the street. Leave now and don't come back."

Tommy turned to leave, but a man standing at the counter waiting to pay for a large stack of fruits and vegetables tossed him two apples and flipped a coin to the shopkeeper in payment.

"Thanks, mister!"

The merchant turned to the customer and said, "You shouldn't encourage them, I don't need street trash in my place."

"I hope you don't need me either, because I won't be back. You can forget about all this stuff I was going to buy."

"But sir, you don't understand, these street kids . . ."

The man slammed the door on his way out.

⊷⟊ ⟊⊶

Eddie tugged on the skirt of a woman working in the bakery and smiled. She asked, "Are you hungry, little boy?"

He nodded yes.

"I got some rolls that are getting a little stale. You want them?"

Another smile and a question. "You got anything to put on them?"

"You're a pushy one, but you're cute." She pinched his cheek and he laughed.

Eddie lowered his head, and then tilted sideways while raising it. He offered a well-choreographed wink and grin out of the right side of his mouth.

"You sure can work that smile! Here you go." She handed him a stick of butter and said, "Please don't start coming around all the time. I can't afford to do this every day."

"Thank you, ma'am." Eddie headed outside and found a spot to hide his bag while he made his last stop, the butcher. He stood quietly in the back with his head down while the man at the counter finished cutting some ham. The man started to clean up the carving area and Eddie cleared his throat as he raised his head. "Sir, I don't mean to bother you, 'cause you're busy and all, but do you think I could have those leftovers? I haven't eaten in a long time." He lowered his head and waited for a response.

The man smiled. He had already bagged up the scraps and added a few decent pieces on top. "Here you go, young man, but you need to understand this is a one-time thing. Off with ya!"

⊷⟊ ⟊⊶

Slobbering Sam had two pears, Fat Franky, a jug of orange juice, and Two-Tooth, just his apples. Tommy looked up, "Here he is, fellas. You're gonna like him."

Triple N rushed over and displayed the contents of his bag. Franky stated the obvious, "Ham sandwiches! How the hell did you get all this grub!" Sam patted his new friend on the back and took out his knife to spread the butter. Franky placed the meat inside the rolls and Tommy cut up the fruit. The boys passed around the jug as they laughed, ate, and enjoyed each other's company.

The feast came to an end and the newsies headed back to their corners. Two-Tooth put his arm around Triple N as they walked toward the ferry. "So how do you like the newspaper business?" Eddie smiled and started to run. "Race you to the corner." Tommy began a slow jog and arrived well after his guttersnipe, who deserved the win.

CHAPTER 9

Where the Hell is Tangiers?

SILVY ORGANIZED THE unsettled invoices and the full week's issues of the *Sun* on one of the tables toward the front and warned his new worker, "Your first day will be the hardest because both the statements and newspapers piled up during the week." Bodee contained his smile. *This job isn't so bad at all—he thinks this is hard? All I need to do is sit inside, push some papers, and read for a spell.*

"Your grandmother and me spoke about you. This job will work a certain way—you stay away from the whores next door at Tigress, steer clear of all of the gangsters, and if you talk to anybody, stick to neighborhood people. My plan though, not so involved—only six words. You think you can handle six words, clever boy?"

"I think so."

"Here they are: *get the fuck out before four.* Simple enough."

"Understood."

"The time is one o'clock. Why is this important?"

"Because I need to *get the fuck out before four!*"

"Your first test—I'm going to give you an A. So you are the only employee on the day shift in a night establishment. Can you deal with working alone, Mr. Rivers?"

"I'll manage. You ready for the headlines?"

"Sure am."

Bodee began his review of the major news reports with a sip of coffee before he read each headline. The title of the story floated between the two men until Silvy sipped his coffee and shook his head up and down to read more or side-to-side to move on. Areas of interest included fighting between Japan and Russia in Taiwan and the constant complaints about the World's Fair in St. Louis. Spanish warships and US Marines in Tangiers received both a horizontal nod and a chuckle as both men asked in unison, "Where the hell is Tangiers?"

Another interesting story related to the Brooklyn police. The article quoted the leader of Tammany Hall offering words about responsible, honest governing, which Silvy found to be hilarious. The more thought-provoking part of the story, however, involved a common theme noted in the dailies since the consolidation of New York in 1898—Brooklyn still struggled with the reality it was no longer an independent city. Both men agreed—they liked the local stories best.

After the last side-to-side signal, the new bookkeeper turned his attention to the bills and made plans for payments. A few minutes later, the boss pointed to the clock. "Six words, smart boy. One. Two, three . . ."

They both screamed, "*Get the fuck out before four!*"

Finished for the day, Bodee rushed out of the door, stepping backward as he joked, "Need to go to the *Sun* to complain about the St. Louis World's Fair—like everyone else!"

Bodee backpedaled through the front door, and when he attempted to turn around, he bumped into Arlin McFarland—a new member of the Whyos gang. Bodee's momentum propelled the Irishman into a lamppost, which struck his back with force.

"Sorry, sir, I didn't see you. Let me pick up your hat from the floor."

The tall and heavyset gang member grabbed his fedora with his left hand and shoved Bodee with his right, pushing him back into Snake Eyes and knocking him to the dirt floor. The gangster followed him in, picked up the corner spittoon, and threw it at Bodee's head. Silvy moved in between the two men and McFarland reared back his right hand. The head of the crew, Shamus McTiernan, shouted, "Stop. Enough. Take a step back. We'll sort this out."

Bodee took his time getting up from the floor, went behind the bar, and reached for some ice, which he put in a towel and applied to his head. *I tried to apologize, but if I stand up to these men, they'll break me like a twig. How do I get into these situations! God, this is my first day on the job. I'll stay back here and let Silvy try to fix this.*

Moments later, Blood and a few of the other locals marched through the front door and stood side-by-side with the two Snake Eyes employees, who both shared a sigh of relief. McFarland advanced while his mates retreated. The gang leader instructed, "I said no more. Move back." McFarland liked the odds, and thought less of his new colleagues, who didn't have the balls to take on a couple of Darkeys.

Silvy tried to take control. "No harm here. Not done on purpose—lots of legitimate fights on Minetta Lane, boys, but this ain't one of them. This Juba's boy and he didn't mean to knock into you and he 'pologized. You not hurt and you got a little payback. The boy's all messed up." Silvy glanced back at Bodee, who held the towel filled with ice cubes to his head.

"Listen, old man, if you think this is fucked up, you need a lesson on the subject and I'll be happy to teach both him and you. Not going to be too hard with this skinny piece of shit. Nobody pushes around Arlin McFarland, and who the hell is Juba?"

Blood reacted to the sign of disrespect to Madame Juba by moving forward with his men until he raised his hand, which caused the entire group to stop their advance.

McFarland's messmates realized they'd neglected to enlighten him about the respectful coexistence of these two ethnic groups in this part of the city as well as the significance of Blood and Juba. The newest Whyo flashed a menacing stare at Blood, who responded with one of his own. No one, other than McFarland, wanted a problem over something as stupid as this. An unspoken truce took hold as Blood and McTiernan exchanged glances and the matter was put to rest. Silvy provided drinks on the house as the final punctuation to the conflict while Bodee slipped out the back door.

Blood called McTiernan to the back of the bar. "Shamus, the boy is Juba's grandson. Nothing happens to him. Explain how things work to your new man. He better learn how to show respect—better for you to school him than me." McTiernan stared back at Blood, but did not acknowledge his comment or respond at first. A quick response of assurance would have been extended if Blood omitted his last line—no Black could threaten a Whyo, not even Blood.

"Slow down that kind of talk. I'll let you slide this time, but you can't go threatening a Whyo, even a new guy who don't understand the rules yet. He just got here from Chicago. I'll school him, but you better back the fuck up." Blood took his own sweet time before moving back and the little game of power and positioning came to an end.

⊷═◉ ◉═⊷

"Juba, something bad happened at work today."

"I'm happy you came right over to tell me, but I know already. You need to be careful around the Whyos. Sounds like you were foolin' around—that kind of thing can get you killed around here. Time to be serious, but don't worry, we'll make this go away."

"Hard to believe—my first day."

"Welcome to the Bend! Let's not make too much of this—Black and Irish have spats from time to time. Some people demand respect—on the Black side, it's me and Blood—you too, because you connected to me."

"Why do you have so much power?"

"That's a story for another day. For now, understand that the Whyos are at war all over downtown and they don't need problems where they come at night to relax and drink. We all live by a code that everybody understands and follows. Guessing I know it better than anyone."

"How come?"

"I wrote it."

CHAPTER 10

The Whyos

SHAMUS MCTIERNAN RAN one of the best and highest-earning Whyo crews. The men were all handpicked with one notable exception, Arlin McFarland, who became a member as a favor to one of the senior bosses. At the end of day one on the crew, the Chicago transplant demonstrated an uncontrollable temper, a poor work ethic, and an inability to understand the ways of the gang, but he had a fury and a viciousness that was rare even among a group as sadistic as the Whyos. With some tips and mentoring, Shamus thought he might still be a good addition—the tutoring would continue.

The men sat around a long table with glasses of their favorite Irish whiskey. Shamus cleared his throat as he poured their second round. "The song, 'Finnegan's Wake,' in the key of C sounds like this . . ." The singing commenced and the leader, turned conductor, motioned with his arms to "cut," and the music halted. "This means everything is fine, stick with the plan, but if we switch to the key of D—things aren't going right . . ." McTiernan's hands came down and the song continued, but only for a few bars. He asked, "Understand?"

"Ain't no difference at all. What does 'Finnegan's Wake' have to do with busting heads? I got no idea what you're talking about. The key of C and the key of D? What the hell is that? How many more of these stupid signals are you going to show me?"

McTiernan reached his limit. He had struggled all day to keep his cool. Now that they returned to the privacy of their headquarters, it was time to set the new guy straight. He turned to Jimmy McPhee, his most long-term man. "Jimmy. Take the other boys with ya and leave me alone with the new lad for a wee bit— we need to chat. One more drink for the road, boys?"

"Sure thing, boss."

McTiernan changed his mind as the men finished their drinks, "No, wait. Let's do one last thing before you go. All Whyos need to understand how we roll the cheer and the war cry all up into one. Let's to do that together." The four men started with a whisper, and progressed to chant of "Why-o, Why-o, Why-o" in a one-two rhythm. Their voices blended into a chord as the men found their natural melodic positions—McTiernan was the base. The eerie war cry confused the tone-deaf McFarland. After a few minutes, he tried to join in, but was so off-key several of the gang members gestured for him to stop as they brought the last "Why-o" to its logical musical conclusion and headed out of the building.

"Listen, Arlin, you're used to the Chicago way, but you're in New York and things work different here. These signals keep us together and out of jail. We train on seven of them, but since you're as tone deaf as my Grandma Fiona, I'll give you a pass and we'll remember you can never be alone. By the way, we would all appreciate it if you just moved your lips during the battle cry."

"McTiernan, this is such bullshit—singing to be in a gang? What kind of pansies are ya? Back in Chicago, I'd shit on sissy singing girls like you, and it wouldn't matter a lick whether we were in the scale of V or Z, or whatever the hell you said."

The leader took a deep breath and walked over to his new messmate. With one movement, he slammed McFarland's head to the table, and with a second move, McTiernan pressed the business end of a switchblade against the side of the new Whyo's face. "Don't ever speak about fucking Chicago again—you may be somebody's cousin, but you're shit to me. I'm two steps from the top in the Whyos and I'm going higher and you're on the bottom rung and nothing but a tone-deaf hothead. The tone-deaf problem we can work with—you're not the only one, but the pansy comments and all the other shit you been saying stops. Learn the rules . . . don't mouth off to me, and the shit you pulled at Snake Eyes won't ever happen again. The Darkey is protected—he's connected to Madame Juba and Blood. They run things in the Bend. Don't touch a hair on his skinny Black head. Do you understand me?"

McFarland nodded and McTiernan released his grip, threw him to the floor, and left the room. Arlin summarized his takeaways for the day. *Screw the Whyos, their pansy signals, and their rules. Arlin McFarland doesn't forgive and forget—he gets even. The little Darkey will pay, and Shamus McTiernan will get his melodious ass kicked in the near future in the popular scale of fuck you.*

CHAPTER 11

Helmut

BODEE BEGAN HIS walk hoping some fresh air would clear his mind. A young White man stood at the intersection of Minetta and Sixth, checking something written on a piece of paper. The man wore a full suit with a necktie and the shiniest black shoes Bodee had ever seen. Whispers were exchanged by the thugs in wait behind concealed basement doors . . . *come on down* . . . *got something for ya* . . . *right over here.* The code was clear-cut, but unfair—the man wasn't drunk or looking for any kind of trouble, but he was White, and therefore fair game. The mumbling in the shadows increased as Blood's cast of villains negotiated the composition of the neighborhood welcoming party.

Bodee hoped the man would play along as he approached. "Hi, how are you? Happy you had the time to come down. The place I wanted to show you is up on the avenue. Right this way." The man turned to check if someone else was the intended recipient of this greeting. Bodee acted as if he tripped and when he fell toward the man, he whispered, "If you keep walking the way you're going, you'll be attacked. Follow me."

"Ah, yes. I thought I might be headed the wrong way," the man said. "How are you?"

"Fine. This way."

"Listen, this is the worst block in New York," Bodee said. "So if you need to go somewhere on the other side, you go in the daytime and you walk around Minetta. White people are robbed around here all the time. You were about to be next."

"Thank you so much for your help. I didn't understand all of that, but I do now. My name is Helmut Wagner and I live in Kleindeutschland, which you might call Little Germany. You can use either name."

"What did you say? Kleindoland?"

"I see we have to work on your accent. It isn't Kleindoland, but you got the Klein part right. It is Klein—deutch—land."

"Klein—deutch—land."

"You got it. Your first German word! It might be easier for you to say Little Germany."

"Little Germany it is."

"Not so far from here. Some of the best food and beer in the city. You're right, by the way, I wanted to go to the other side of this neighborhood to run an errand for my church. I appreciate you looking out for me."

"Happy to help. I would have felt guilty if you got robbed. My name is Bodee Rivers."

Helmut extended his hand and Bodee paused for a moment. *A White man shaking the hand of a Black man he just met in public? Interesting.*

"Nice to meet you," Helmut said. "Sometimes I don't pay attention—I'm so caught up in my work with St. Mark's. I'm a volunteer, but one day I hope to be a reverend. First, I need to enroll in the seminary." Helmut paused, looked up at a passing bird, and smiled. "Bodee, do you know where Tomkins Square Park is?"

"Yes, but you shouldn't be walking around so much, I—"

"You must think I have no idea how to survive in the city, but I'm not going there now and not suggesting you go either. St. Mark's is having an outdoor function at Tomkins on Saturday around two. We'll have plenty of good music and delicious food."

"I don't tend to be welcome in mixed crowds, but I'm grateful for the invitation. Anyway, I think I'm going to be spending all of my free time looking for work. The first day of my new job didn't go so well today."

"I may have an idea for you, if you're interested in a summer job."

"I am interested, but I just met you, Mr. Wagner—why would you do this for me?"

"Let's get one thing straight—you and I are about the same age. No more of this Mr. Wagner. Helmut is fine. Mr. *Anything* makes me sound like an old man."

"You're definitely not an old man. Tell me about the job."

"Well, I think you should apply for work on one of the Knickerbocker steamships in Manhattan. This company does daily excursions on boats from both the east side and west side. The man who does the hiring is a friend of mine and he owes me a favor. They need help in the summer when they're busy. Interested?"

"For sure!" Bodee shook the hand of his first White friend, and asked, "How do I submit my application?"

"Through me."

"What do you mean?"

"It is important for me to personally introduce you. Meet me Saturday morning at the east side docks around seven. Helmut took out his notepad, scribbled the address, and handed it to Bodee. I'll make the introductions and make sure things go well. My friend will like you, not to worry. Who knows, you might still be able to make the picnic!"

"See you at seven on Saturday and thanks for your help. I'm heading out, but remember, stay away from Minetta Lane."

"Got it! Excellent advice!"

CHAPTER 12

The Newsboys Lodging House

"YOU DID OKAY today, Triple N, but since it's Thursday, we need to get beds at the Newsboys Lodging House—they serving pork 'n' beans, my favorite. Right down the block." Tommy pointed. "Corner of Duane and Chambers. Like before. Do what I do."

"Welcome. You're in time for supper!" A staff member announced to the five or six newsies who arrived together. The boys climbed the stairs to the second floor and entered the long dining room, which seated two hundred.

Tommy whispered, "See—free food. Thursday night's the best." We can sit together when we eating, but not during school."

"What do you mean, school?"

"All right. Let me explain. You can eat if you check in before seven, like we did, but school comes next 'til nine. They might split us up, because I'm one of the biggest kids. Makes no difference to me which class I'm in because I don't even know what I don't know. Not really sure what that means, but you get my problem. I can try to go with the little kids, but they'll stop me. Understand?"

"So what happens after school?

"I'll tell you later, time for dinner . . . the line is forming up, hurry."

Eddie neared the end of his first few decent days since his father had gone away. Two-Tooth had taught him how to make money and brought him to a place with food and a bed. In order to stay close, Eddie cut the line and squeezed in behind his new friend. The kid he cut elbowed him in return, but Tommy's directed scowl provided an acceptable resolution to the matter. "Make sure everyone understands you're with Two-Tooth and they won't fuck with you," Tommy said.

The boys walked up to the third floor after finishing their food and one of the matrons asked each child to stand next to a line drawn on the wall. Those below the mark went with the young kids, and those above went with the bigger boys. The same separation of groups applied to the dormitories. Triple N glanced up at the line and did the only sensible thing—he stood on his toes. The matron picked up her paddle and smacked him on the butt. "Ah, you want to play games, do you? Heels down. With the little ones, dearie. You'll need a whole lot more pork 'n' beans before you'll be in the other group."

One of the other short children, who sported some whiskers on his face, walked over, and said, "Yes, *dearie*, more pork 'n' beans. Maybe I'll give you some of mine later." The boy's taunting stopped as Tommy approached slowly—anyone who ran or caused a disruption lost privileges for the night and found themselves back on the street.

"Stay clear of him, Triple N. He's my age, but he's short and likes to be with the smaller kids so he can do stuff. Stay away."

"Okay, Tommy."

School started with a lesson about the alphabet. Eddie's mind wandered— his job involved selling papers, not reading them, and he put his head down on his desk. His dream took him back to his last birthday, when his dad came home with a cake and told him one day his thousand-dollar smile would make him successful in life. The smile started in the soles of his feet and traveled all the way to his face. He worked his smile for his dad like a professional model—happy, sarcastic, funny—all the ways Dad liked it. The instructor walked toward Eddie's seat and slapped the back of his desk with her paddle as his smile came into full bloom. The boys erupted in laughter. The teacher moved closer to his desk and leaned down. "School until nine, bed comes last. Wipe the smile off your face and stop dreaming about perverted things, you little deviant!"

"Yes, ma'am," he cried. *What is perverted? What does deviant mean?* He smiled again as he thought, *I'm like Two-Tooth, I don't even know what I don't know.* He laughed and she hit him again. The boy with the whiskers smiled.

Another boy whispered to Eddie, "You in trouble tonight. Better keep something in your hand to protect yourself. Tommy can't help you down here."

School ended at nine and the boys marched upstairs to the dormitories, where the instructor was again in charge. She glowered at him. "I better not hear a peep from you."

The boys put all belongings, other than their shirt and pants, in secured lockers and received their bed locations. Eddie sat on bed #10 and noted his bearded nemesis at #15. Most of the newsies woke up between two and five in the morning and headed down to Newspaper Row for their stacks of papers for the next day, so everyone settled down without much of a fuss at bedtime. The boy with the stubble walked over. "I'll be coming over to you later, and if you're quiet, I won't hurt you."

"Lights out in five minutes," the matron proclaimed as she began her final walk-through of the dorm for the guttersnipes, the weaker newsies who needed extra protection. The Street Arabs, who either took care of or abused their weaker counterparts, slept on the floor below. She needed to check if any Street Arab had snuck in. The bearded boy turned onto his stomach when she passed by, and from this position, he fit the profile.

The boys folded their trousers and shirts, put them under their mattresses, and got under the covers for bed. Triple N didn't remove any of his clothes and lay on his back, clutching the ruler he'd swiped earlier from the matron's desk. He wanted to sleep, but understood his predicament and needed to stay alert. Minutes after his eyelids closed, he felt a hand over his mouth. "Like I said, if you don't make noise, this goes much better for you. You might like it."

Eddie scrambled to find his improvised weapon with his right hand, while he punched his attacker with his left. The boy laughed, "This is going to be easier than I thought," as he stuck a sock deep in Eddie's mouth. The sock muffled his cries better than the hand. Another left-handed punch from Eddie, and another laugh from the attacker. Eddie's right hand was still searching.

His attacker turned up the intensity and delivered several abdominal punches before flipping Eddie onto his stomach, face down on the bed. The searching continued, but punching was no longer an option. The attacker relaxed his grip when the thrashing decreased and pulled Eddie's pants down to his ankles. The flailing came to a complete halt and the boy smiled.

Eddie felt the edge of the ruler as his hand swept under the bed. Once he was sure he had the proper grip, he flipped over and plunged the sharp end of his makeshift knife into his attacker's midsection. A piercing scream woke up everyone in the vicinity and someone began ringing a bell. Eddie removed the sock from his mouth, pulled his pants up, and sat on the edge of the bed. The boy fell to the floor with the piece of wood still lodged in his abdomen.

Staff came running from the surrounding rooms to investigate. A few minutes later, two attendants carried the bleeding boy into the lobby and later to the hospital. Eddie collected his things and reported to the office to meet with the head of the facility.

The superintendent opened the conversation. "What's your name? Don't give me some crazy nickname. I want your real name."

"Edward Murphy Junior."

"Excuse us for one minute, Edward. I need to speak with Mrs. Eastman for a moment." Once outside in the hallway, he asked, "Why do you think this tiny boy is involved with some kind of perversion? He's not more than eight years old. I'm not sure he comprehends what an impure thought is."

"I'm tellin' you—seen this before. This child is going straight to hell. He lured the other boy to his bed and gored him after they'd had their fun—the work of the devil!"

"All right, the weapon part of this is bad. To be honest, I'm not so sure about all the rest. You tend to accuse a lot of the boys of possessing these impure thoughts, Mrs. Eastman."

"How dare you! Are you questioning my honesty?"

"No, not your honesty, but perhaps your interpretation of events. Put him out. I'm going back to bed."

Mrs. Eastman reentered the office and took the superintendent's seat behind the desk, straightening up some folders as she sat. "You're a bad apple. Where are your parents?"

"My father went on a long trip. Been gone for weeks."

"Your father did not go on a trip, you stupid boy. He recognized your deviant ways and got as far away from you as possible. I'm sure you invited the child you injured into your bed, and after your perverted fun, you attacked him with the ruler you stole from me. You're the devil. This place isn't for you, and don't come back until you repent. Off with ya."

Two staff members ushered him back onto the street. Alone again—all of the progress of the day erased. *Am I really bad? Did something about me make Dad leave? Why did the older boy come after me?* Eddie turned the corner and began to head for his old spot in the alley. A familiar voice called out from a distance. "Wait up. Hold on." Tommy ran toward him.

"You think I'd leave you all by yourself? We're a team. You gave him what he had comin'. Stop your crying, you showed everyone—no one ever gonna mess with you again!" Tommy picked up a broomstick from the gutter and started making stabbing movements as he continued, "Most important thing is we got the pork 'n' beans." The two boys raced the three blocks. Tommy let Eddie win and within minutes of arriving home, they crawled into their spots behind the crate and fell asleep.

Chapter 13

Knickerbocker

"Thanks for doing this, Helmut. Am I ruining your Saturday?"

"No, not at all, Bodee. I still have enough time to prepare for the church function. Here comes my friend."

"Audrick, how are you? This is the person I told you about who wants to work on one of your steamers."

"You didn't tell me he's a Darkey."

Didn't see that coming, Helmut thought. "Bodee, I need to mention one thing to Audrick before the two of you talk. Would you mind giving us a minute?"

"Sure. I'll be over by the railing."

The two men waited in an awkward silence as Bodee moved away. Helmut began the conversation. "Funny thing . . . I think there may be a pattern here. You're right, I did forget to tell you the color of his skin, and I think I also forgot to tell your wife that I ran into you with a whore out on the town the other night. I sure do forget many things."

"All right, no need for that kind of talk. I was surprised is all. We hire Blacks for some of the positions and this fella can help me save money because Coloreds make half as much as Whites—so this is a good thing! Tell him to come back over."

"No, let me speak to him first and then the two of you can work out the details."

Helmut smiled as he walked toward the railing. "Bodee, I'm leaving—you'll be fine. The salary may not be the best, but it's something and you'll be outside in the fresh air—not too bad for the summer. St. Mark's rented a ship through Knickerbocker as transportation for our annual getaway, so depending on where they assign you, I may be with you on Wednesday. Got to run to the church for services, but if you need me, this is my address—not too far from you."

"I appreciate what you done. Thanks."

"You did a favor for me and now I did one for you. Oh, don't forget about later, Tomkins Square Park, two p.m. I'm counting on you!"

"I'll try my best."

⊸—◉ ◉—⊷

The hiring manager outlined the details of the position to Bodee, who agreed with Helmut's assessment—the wages weren't much as a Black porter, but he would begin right away. Audrick explained that he could complete his employee forms over the next few days and start in the meanwhile. He was escorted to the gangway of the Knickerbocker vessel docked at the same location and handed off to a man standing by the entrance.

"Welcome aboard. This is the *SS Grand Republic* and I'm the first mate. You can call me Gilbride. The captain is John Pease, but if you have any issues, come to me and leave him be. You can say hello to him, but remember, come to me with any questions or problems."

"Yes, sir. Come to you."

"The crew is about thirty-five strong, doing different kinds of work depending on whether we're at the pier or on an excursion. The *SS Grand Republic* is one of the classic steamboats in New York—the best in every way when we launched in 1878, but in 1904, most boats are newer, some faster, and a few a little fancier. We're still top-notch, though, and believe me, we're plenty fancy, but we spend most of our time maintaining appearances. Things always need to look sharp. One of our jobs today is to 'slush down' the wood because it dries out over time. The slush is a mixture of turpentine and linseed oil and it keeps the wood in tip-top shape. We provide new coats of paint on a regular basis and we do touch-ups all the time—that's what we're doing later this morning. This is Duane, the head porter. He'll set you up to work a couple of hours today, and you'll start full-time on Monday."

"Yes, sir. Thanks so much for the job."

A young Colored man walked over and introduced himself. "My name is Duane. You Bodee?"

"Yeah."

"Pleased to meet you. We two of seven Colored staff. They let us do the grunt work and don't pay us like the Whites, but they leave us alone. Not bad work during the summer."

"Yeah, fresh air and all."

"Not as much as you might like. Most times we're down below in the lamp room or the engine room when we're not in the restaurant. I'll show you where everything is. We'll do the walk-through before we start the touch-ups. You should be out of here by noon."

"I'm supposed to go to a picnic at two in the park. The time works real well."

"Okay, great. Did the hiring manager say you could fill out the payroll stuff over the next few days?"

"Yeah, he did."

"This means everything you do until then is for no pay. They do this to all of the Black folk who get hired. I worked for almost a week until I filled out my papers, so I'll try to schedule you for only a few hours until you do yours. Let me keep telling you about the boat . . . we can hold up to twenty-five hundred people. We'll start the walk-through with the two large open areas we call salons on the lower and middle decks."

Bodee admired the way the sunlight from the massive windows highlighted the blue velvet on the upholstered wicker chairs as he walked through the middle salon. The hurricane deck sat above the salons and measured ten thousand square feet of open space enclosed only by a short, three-foot high railing. Two tall smokestacks towered above the upper level and massive paddle wheels occupied both the front and rear.

"You seen everything now except down below. Follow me."

Bodee turned toward the stairs and took note of the swinging door to the service area, which was stuck in a halfway open position with the ship's name painted in brown letters on a white background with only the *SS* portion of the name visible. The door and lettering appeared familiar. He stopped to think as his eyes continued to focus on the door. Duane's voice became background noise as he entered his dream. The door was within view and . . .

Duane tapped Bodee on the shoulder. "You okay? Did you hear what I said? We need to go. You all right? Thought I lost you for a minute."

"Yeah, I'm fine. Had the feeling I been here before. Ever happen to you?"

"No. Don't think so. Let's finish up."

The men entered the engine room and received a nod from a mechanic tinkering with a gauge. "The *Republic*'s body may be old, but its heart is brand new! This here is the best steam engine money can buy, made by W. & A. Fletcher, and these two boilers and this here coal keeps it moving. Sometimes, you'll shovel the coal. Come on, one last stop."

"This is the lamp room and I start out here every morning. I light the lamps on each of the decks. We store other things in here, though, so you might need to come down to pick up some varnish or something. Tour is over. Time for work."

After a few minutes, Bodee realized the door on the upper deck was an image from a repetitive dream he'd had over the years. Ever since he moved in with Juba, the images became brighter and easier to make out. During his first night on Minetta Lane, the vision was clear enough to see two letters on the left-hand side of the door, but the letters were fuzzy. *Could have been SS*, Bodee thought.

Duane clapped his hands. "I won't say nothing to the boss, but I keep losing you. You a daydreamer or something? Better stay away from Gilbride. Take this paint and touch up any cracks you find around the lifeboats. Climb down using the rope ladder and don't worry, the lifeboats are steady—they chained them to the sides years ago because the jiggling noises bothered the passengers. Start painting and stop all the daydreaming, so you can be out of here by noon."

Bodee enjoyed the solitary painting work and reflected on his new job on the steamship. The crew got along well and did their best to cover up the fact that the boat's finest years were in the past. Tremendous amounts of paint and varnish were applied in multiple layers. *After all of these years, the ship must be more varnish than wood! The old girl better have one last summer left in her.* He was quite sure she did.

CHAPTER 14

Saturday in the Park

"HELMUT, WHY DID the reverend let you talk him into this picnic today? We have two grand events next week. First, the Schuetzen Bund Parade on Monday. Everyone will be at the reviewing stand, including the mayor, and then the annual St. Mark's outing is also next week. Too much all at once. Why do you spend your time with this? Don't you understand I need you in the shop? The Wagners are butchers, not preachers. Stop all of this foolishness and cancel this picnic if the turnout is poor—you're in charge, so be the boss!"

Helmut interrupted—his father delivered this speech at least three times a week since he had finished high school two years ago. Slicing meat never factored into Helmut's plans. Volunteering at St. Mark's Evangelical Lutheran Church provided a sense of purpose more important than anything he might accomplish as a butcher. "Father, I understand your position on these matters. Today, we will celebrate and if the numbers are small, there will be more hot dogs and beer for everyone!"

His father smiled. "I can't be mad at you. How can I help?"

"Thank you. The problem at the moment is the band—they cancelled at the last minute." Helmut spotted at least ten members of the choir among the first fifty parishioners. After a quick consultation, they began a rousing version of a popular song and the party started.

Our God is a secure fortress,
a good shield and weapon;
He helps us willingly out of all troubles,
that now have encountered us.
The old, evil enemy

is earnestly bent on it,
great strength and much deceit
are his horrid armaments,
there is nothing like him on earth.

⊷▬⊙ ⊙▬⊶

Bodee entered Tomkins Square Park and headed toward the source of the singing. *Not sure this is German, but it sure ain't English.* He came within twenty feet of the crowd, but didn't see his new friend. Most of the St. Mark's flock stood around clapping their hands, but two groups separated from the pack—four men chatting and smoking cigars, and several giggling teenage girls. The men flashed Bodee a collective sneer and began an animated dialogue.

"What is this Black man doing here?"

"He's looking at those girls. We can't have this, let's go tell him to move on."

"Yes, let's do that. This is the danger of America, we must protect our women."

"He has to go. Let's walk over and tell the Black man to move on."

None of the men moved toward Bodee, but assembled in a line as if their strong message demanded a particular formation. The giggling from the girls stopped as the men presented their longest and most sustained stare. Helmut arrived just in time.

"Welcome everyone. Today will be a fine day for St. Mark's. What perfect weather! Don't you agree, gentlemen?"

"Why, yes, but we need to tell this Black man—"

"Oh, so sorry. Allow me to introduce you. This is my friend. I invited him today."

The most vocal of the four men leaned toward Helmut and whispered, "You invited a Black man to a church function? We can't have Blacks diluting the blood of good Germans, and it all starts with inviting them to a picnic. Tell him to go."

Helmut turned to Bodee. "This fine gentlemen told me that he remembered how nice it felt when he came to this country and other groups welcomed him with open arms. He mentioned that even though this was only a short while ago, sometimes it is easy to forget. All of the men extend their warmest greetings and hope you enjoy the day as our guest."

The men grunted, turned, and went back to their original location. One called back. "Du denkst, du bist so schlau. Sie ihn besser Fernhalten von Mädchen, oder sehen Sie, wie willkommen er ist. *You think you're so smart. You better keep him away from the girls, or you'll see how welcome he is.*"

"Do you want me to leave?"

"Don't worry about them. Stay by my side. Other church members may be more accepting. In any case, I'm so happy you came."

⊷▬◉ ◉▬⊶

Helmut first noticed the small child in an oversized shirt crouching behind a bush toward the end of the stimulating chorale performance. The youngster ran out from his hiding place when the cook turned away from the barbecue, and he dashed back when the cook returned his attention to the grill. Many of the picnickers started to laugh at this humorous little boy with such exceptional taste in food. Helmut walked over, hot dog in hand, and tapped the boy on the shoulder. "Guten tag, is this what you want?" Helmut extended his hand and offered a hot dog, fresh from the grill, and the boy offered his most beautiful smile in return. The onlookers applauded.

"You got one more of those for me?"

Helmut looked up and found Bodee hovering over his shoulder. "Sure do." The photographer hired for the day noted the interesting photo opportunity and snapped a shot of Eddie biting his hot dog, with Helmut on one knee by his side and Bodee leaning down over them. Smiles abounded, but Eddie stole the show.

"What's your name, little man?" Helmut inquired.

"My real name is Edward Murphy Junior, but they call me Triple N at work."

"At work? What do you do?" Bodee asked.

"I'm a newspaperman. My name is about the business. I'm the No Neck Newsie—Triple N." Eddie waved his hand inside the excess room in the collar of his father's shirt. "Get it?"

Both men laughed and Helmut said, "Yeah, the name fits! I'm your host today. My name is Helmut Wagner and I'm with St. Mark's."

"And I'm Bodee Rivers. I helped Mr. Wagner out of a tight spot the other day."

"I'm always in a tight spot," Eddie added as the group of women who gathered around the hot dog-eating boy *oohed and aahed* at his every remark. At one point he asked, "Who do I talk to about bein' German? Want me more of those hot dogs!" His audience swooned once more.

"Such a cute boy!"

"So funny!"

Eddie, fully in the moment, put on his best routine and ate the last few crumbs of bun off his fingers. "Delissious, I tell ya!" The sun peeked out from behind a cloud and the rays felt so warm on his face another smile emerged, but it all ended as it always did. *Why do they always ask the same thing?*

"Where are your parents, little boy?"

Eddie never handled this question well—there was no acceptable answer and nowhere to go with the conversation after it was asked. He tucked his smile away for the day and sat on the ground with his head down. Eventually, he curled up in a ball and fashioned himself a turtle and refused to leave his shell until everyone left. After some time, the chatter stopped, but he wasn't alone. One person remained—a woman with a kind face. She asked, "Are you okay?" as she extended her arms toward Eddie. He glanced to his left and right—it was just the two of them—and he dug in for his first hug since his mother had passed away five years earlier.

⇥▰ ▰⇤

Bodee walked to a different part of Tompkins Square to sit and think of his excellent fortune—every time one door closed, another opened. The sun snuck out again when a beautiful girl with a flowery summer dress took a seat two benches away. Bodee caught a hint of a smile on her face and that's all the encouragement he needed. For some reason, he bowed when in front of her and said, "My name is Bodee Rivers. I see you holding a book. Don't suppose this book tells you where Tangiers is, because there's lots of stuff happening over there. Spanish ships, US marines, you name it. Read about everything in the *Sun* today." *How stupid. Why am I asking this girl about Tangiers and why am I bowing?* He slapped himself on the side of the head.

The girl laughed and flashed the whitest teeth Bodee had ever seen in his life. "No need to slap yourself anymore, Bodee Rivers. My name is Nellie Washington and this here book don't have nothing to do with Tangiers, which I think is in Africa, and why you bowing at me like I'm some kind of princess? Come over here and sit down. Tell me about these newspapers you been reading."

The conversation continued for the rest of the afternoon and Bodee walked her home with the promise they would meet in the same spot on Monday night. *Bad leads to good. Closed doors mean you keep walking 'til you find another one that's open. Everything happens for a reason.* Bodee's takeaways from his last few days were numerous and profound. He climbed into his cot and gave thanks for his recent gifts: his new friend, Helmut, his first hot dog, and the introduction to someone who might prove to be the love of his life. *Not a bad day.*

CHAPTER 15

Time to Tell

BODEE ROLLED OVER and opened his eyes. He was on the ship. A little girl dropped to her knees by the door with the painted "SS" and started to pray. She glanced at Bodee, who understood she needed help, but she wasn't within reach. The blinding light overwhelmed him. He looked up and the girl was gone, but then she was back. Bodee held his sleeve up to his eyes and rubbed them as he continued to move toward the girl. Her solemn prayers were drowned out by joyous music and laughter coming from another direction. The girl was in trouble. *How can others be celebrating?* He needed to make his way to the door and he called out, "It's too bright, turn it down, stop the light." Bodee woke up in a sweat, but when he opened his eyes, what followed wasn't blinding light, but the utter darkness of the middle of the night. Juba sat across from him with her arms folded on her lap. Bodee took a moment and rubbed his eyes in an effort to gain his bearings. "What . . . what's going on here?"

Juba answered. "Tell me about the light. What happened?"

"The light blinded me, burned my eyes. I went to the door because of the little girl. My God, it was terrible!" Bodee's head bopped up and down in rapid succession. "Why are you watching me sleep, Juba? What's goin' on here!"

"This my house and I'll sit wherever I want, and do and watch whatever I want. Tell me about your dream. Who is this girl and is this the first time you seen her?"

"I dreamt the same thing for years. At first, I was far away from the door. I asked Mama, but she said don't bother with nonsense—dreams nothing but nonsense."

"So what changed? Why did the light frighten you? And the girl—tell me about her."

He paused and turned to the wall. "Nothing more than a bad dream. Go back to bed. Sorry for waking you."

"You been doing this every night. Your vision been moving along fast, as far as I can tell. Something must've happened, and don't tell me nothing—because something happened. Remember, I keep telling you that I'll tell when you tell, and I'm not changin' my mind. Time to tell me about these dreams."

"Mama said this all foolishness and not to pay no mind."

"Did you ever hear the sound of a fancy orchestra playing a long piece of music? It's one of the greatest things on earth. They all got these sheets of paper with music symbols that don't mean nothing to most people, but the few who been taught to read them. Your dreams were like those symbols to Akua, made no sense at all, but I understand. Tell me. You tell first."

"Mama got upset when I told her about my dreams. She sometimes mentioned you and said this nothing but Voudou black magic—always a bad conversation, so I only told her every once and a while, and only if they involved real things and people."

"You not disrespecting Akua by telling me now. She couldn't understand, but I do. I want you to tell me."

Bodee rose from his cot, walked over to the pitcher of water on the table, and poured himself a glass. He started to throw on his clothes as well, but she stopped him. "I held you when you a buck-naked child. Don't need no pants, come on over here with those skinny long legs and tell me about the dream."

"All right, time to tell." Bodee took a few moments to figure out where to start. "I started having dreams at about the age of ten. At first, I got up sudden like and thought something happened, but couldn't remember any details. Each time the story moved forward, I'd not only remember the end, but also more of the beginning. Like in a baseball game, I didn't realize I was playin' until the fifth inning, and when I did, I didn't remember how things started, but by the ninth inning, I could tell you what happened all the way back to the first pitch. I had lots of dreams and most didn't make any sense to me, but I did have five or six I needed to talk to Mama about. Like I said, those conversations never went well."

"What made these dreams so important?"

"They involved real things and people where I knew what would happen."

"Now we're getting somewhere, Bodee. Did you get things right in the end?"

"Kind of yes, but sometimes not the way I thought—I didn't put the dream together the right way."

"This is what I want you to do. Tell me about one of the five or six times when you were only kind of right."

"I'll tell you about the one that got me into trouble at school. The teacher gave us this long writing assignment, and they planned to make a fuss over who wrote the best essay. They told us close to the end of my last year when I had practices after school with the Brooklyn Monitors, the team I told about. The way I figured, about half the students were smarter than me, so if I didn't have the time for the project, it wasn't going to be any big loss. The principal said if we didn't do the work, we wouldn't graduate, but I had a dream where I graduated with everyone else. Remember, it the last month of school and I didn't have the time, so I didn't do the assignment."

"What happened?"

"I did graduate, so I was right about that part, but this is where I got things wrong. They still made me come in for two weeks after graduation to do the missing work. I also didn't get picked for the professional team. Nothing worked out the way I wanted. I understood, though, that what I dreamt did happen, but I put the pieces together wrong."

"Putting pieces together is the right way to think of what we doin' here. Tell me about the vision from last night again, but go back to the first time."

"This one took so long to finish up. Started when I was about sixteen, with me standing in a large, dark room with a half-open door at the other end with light coming through. The only light in the room came from the door—that's how it began, but I didn't remember the beginning so well until I started getting closer to the door and the room became clear—a low railing went around each side with some black chairs and tables. The center table had a gold cloth covering and all of the other tabletops were bare. Not such an exciting dream, but it kept coming back every once and a while, which never happened before. Soon after I came to the Bend, the dream moved forward again and I made out some partial letters on the door—just two, SS."

"What happened yesterday?"

"It took me a few minutes to put everything together, but during the first day of my job on the steamship, I actually walked into the room I saw all of these years in my dreams. The room isn't a room at all, it's the hurricane deck—the top level of the ship I started working on. I saw the letters on the door—*SS Grand Republic*. The furniture was different, actually, there was no furniture at all—just a big room with the railing. I guess that's nothing more than a detail."

"Did you go through the door?"

"No."

"Why not?"

"Not sure. I guess I was confused."

"What happened just now?"

"I was on the hurricane deck, but not alone. A crowd of people filled the room and the light coming through the door blinded me and everyone else, except this little girl who got down on her knees and started praying."

"Thanks for telling me. Sometimes saying things out loud helps. We'll figure out what all this means. Seems like you supposed to be on this boat. I'm not sure yet what advice to give you. Let me hold your hands for a spell."

Juba clutched her grandson's hands and took a deep breath. After about a minute, she slowly released them. "Let me ask you something . . . remember the other day, when you pulled me back right before the dirty water came flying out of the window?"

"Yes."

"Why did you do that in such a sudden way?"

"Somehow, I knew the barbershop sign was bad—maybe from another dream, not sure, but I sensed some type of problem, and moved you out of the way."

"I thought as much. Think carefully before you answer this next question. Are you sure you didn't sense the same kind of thing last night?"

"Yes. Nothing bad for me, but the girl was in trouble."

"If you start to feel like you are in danger, stay off the boat and find another job, but as long as you safe, you got to focus on figuring this out. Try to walk through the door today. We need some answers."

"Why you worried so much about this? Like my mother said, nothing but nonsense. I don't think any of this matters."

"You wrong. It does matter. Remember how I told you about your grand-daddy, with the same name as you?"

"Of course I do."

"Well, you alike in many ways—he had dreams too. I planned to wait to explain, but I think I'll tell you now. Put some pants on and come downstairs to the table. I'll go down first. Give me a few minutes."

Bodee wondered if he made a mistake sharing all of this with his grandmother. What difference did it make if he had dreams about light coming through a door? Still, he did as he was told and got dressed. Bodee headed down to the parlor—for what, he didn't know.

CHAPTER 16

The Third Eye

BODEE THOUGHT OF Juba's session with the man who needed advice about his wife. *I wonder if she is going to be* for real *with me.* She was seated at the small table in the center of the room and her guttural moan became audible as he approached. "Hmmm . . . hmmmm."

Bodee thought, *Damn, what she plannin' to do with me? Don't understand how this moaning will help.*

"Sit across from me, and give me your hands."

Bodee eased into his seat and extended his hands to his grandmother, who laced her fingers into his, lowered her head, and began alternating between a whine, a whimper, and a wail—when it stopped, the silence was deafening. He squirmed while she stared. Finally, she released his hands and reached for a glass of water. "My daddy's gift was like yours—he didn't feel things like I do, he saw things like you. One time he tried to show me his way, but you can't teach a blind person to see better by practicing. One thing for sure, you not blind, so I'll show you what my daddy tried to do with me."

"What do you mean? What are we doing here? My mother was right, this is nonsense . . ."

"Shhhhh, enough! You got to trust me. I picked up tremendous energy when I held your hands. You will do something important and you'll need help."

Bodee slumped his shoulders and resolved to persevere through whatever was about to happen. "What do you want me to do?"

"First thing, sit still. Try to be as calm as you can be. You told me about a time when you went to the beach with your high school classmates." He smiled and she continued, "Think of the waves rolling in and drifting out. So quiet, so calm. Are they comin' at you?"

"No, can't see no waves."

"Take your time, relax, Bodee. The waves are coming in and out . . . in and out. Can you see them now?"

"Yeah, yes. I see them now and they keep rolling. So peaceful."

"Excellent. Enjoy the rhythm. Imagine you have a third eye, right in the middle of your forehead. Right here." Juba touched Bodee midway between his eyes and pulled back—the spot, hot to the touch. "I think you ready. Gaze out at the ocean, I want you to locate your steamship. It's waiting for you. Hmmmmmmm . . . hmmmmmmmmm..."

Bodee's breathing slowed and seemed to match the rhythm of Juba's moaning. He no longer saw the candle flame as his eyes closed and other images came into view. He inhaled every time Juba moaned and found their coordinated speech/movements mesmerizing. After a few minutes, he entered into a dreamlike state, which enabled him to listen without being fully present. He closed his eyelids, thinking this would better enable him to open his third eye. His vision took him out to the sea to find the *Republic*. Straight ahead, nothing; to the left, nothing; to the right, a boat in the distance. "I see it—trying to get closer."

Bodee zoomed in and realized it wasn't the *Grand Republic*, but rather a small wooden craft, with ten or twelve distraught people—some cried to themselves, others shrieked to the world, and a few collapsed from the weight of their tears. The unusually hot water splashed and hit Bodee in the face. His arms were so tired. *Not sure I can go on.* He thought of his dismissal from the Brooklyn Monitors and called out, "All speed and no power." *They right, I can't make it.* He gave up and started sinking, just as a man held out an oar as a lifeline.

"Made it." He opened his eyes. Juba released his hands.

"I sensed the swimming as well as the heat. What else happened? Why did you say, 'All speed and no power?'"

"Well, I swam toward a small boat. My arms were so tired. Thought about giving up, but a man dropped the end of the oar into the water and I grabbed onto it. He pulled me up and saved me. The "all speed but no power" thing is what they told me when I wasn't picked for the roster of the baseball team. I think they right, I wasn't strong enough to make it. Thank God for the man on board. I wouldn't have been able to do it on my own."

"Boy, when I hear you sayin' this same 'I can't do it stuff' in a dream, I know it runs deep. You got to change or you'll be no help to no one, including yourself. Did Akua ever tell you about the two parts of your soul?"

"All my religious learning came from the Berean Baptist Church. I guess this is another thing Mama didn't want to talk about."

"Voudou and Christianity mixed a lot over the years and we believe in many of the same things, but we got a twist on the soul. We say there are two different kinds. The first is the *gros bon ange*, which means big good angel, and the second is *ti bon ange*, little good angel. Your *gros bon ange* is potent. This takes care of your body and things you do every day. Probably talent with sports come from this, but you got a problem with your *ti bon ange*."

"What you mean?"

"*Ti bon ange* is where your personality and character come from—this is fine with you. Willpower, though, comes from this as well and this is where you need the most work, but let's go back. Have you seen this boat before?"

"I don't think so. The people were all afraid. They yelled, screamed, and cried. Nothing but confusion."

"What about the room? The one with the railing from last night."

"No room, no hurricane deck, no door, and no steamship—more of a lifeboat."

"Did you sense danger?"

"This time, yes. I worried I couldn't make it. Like I said, the man saved me."

"Bodee, I want you to understand what you just did. When you dream at night, you have no control. You wake up confused and might not even remember everything that happened, but when you learn to use your third eye like I just taught you, you can try to focus on learning what's important. We'll call these visions your daydreams and I want you to practice this whenever you can. Put yourself on the sand lookin' out to the water. Your vision either will take you back to the lifeboat or to the *Republic.* Everything is moving fast. Thing is, we can't be so sure what we're talkin' about—sometimes things might stand for something else, like your graduation dream, so we need to interpret things right."

"Okay. I'll do what you say."

Bodee got up from the table and walked to the back staircase. His experience doing the exercise with his grandmother changed his mind. If he could learn how to direct his daydreams, he might be able to find out something useful. Her words of wisdom about his negative thoughts also rang true. *I'm going live up to my name, just like my granddaddy.*

CHAPTER 17

Gerda Heinrich

"THANKS FOR LETTING me stay here last night and getting me these new clothes, but I'm a little worried—can't lose my nickname. My neck ain't so small when the shirt fits, so I might go with a new name, something German, like Hot Dog. I'll ask Tommy what he thinks, cuz he knows everything, but he say he don't know nothing."

"I enjoyed doing those things for you. I live alone in this apartment."

"Why are you all by yourself, Mrs. Heinrich? Who's the little boy in the picture on the table? Who's the man?"

She reached for the family portrait, held it close to her breast, and said, "Klaus Senior and Junior, who died last year—I miss them so much." Gerda slumped in her chair and used her handkerchief to wipe the tears from her face.

Eddie scanned the apartment and spotted the boy's shoes lined up by the front door and a man's jacket hanging on a coat rack. He glanced again at the photograph and reached out to hold her hand.

"Mrs. Heinrich, don't cry. I don't understand so much about nothing, but I remember how I felt when my mama passed away. You're a nice lady and I'm sorry you're having a rough time."

"Thank you. You're a sweet child."

Eddie jumped out of his chair and peppered his host with questions. "Tell me about them. Was your son a newsie with a funny name? Was your husband a strong man who could lift heavy things like this?" He struggled to pick up one corner of the hefty couch in the living room.

She laughed at first and then the tears returned as she remembered family occasions and moments: Junior's first communion party, Christmas celebrations featuring grand trees that barely squeezed into the apartment, lots of meals to-gether—lots of everything. All gone because of a baseball game and one of those new motor trucks. She thought, *I had a bad feeling that day and I never should have let them go.*

Gerda realized she actually spoke the words when Eddie said, "Where did they go?"

"Hilltop Stadium—they went to opening day for the Highlanders, the new team, in April, last year. My husband and son were both baseball fans. The truck came out of nowhere when they headed home."

"How were you gonna know something like that? Not your fault, but I got to tell ya, I kind of felt that way when my dad sent me out for milk. He never cared so much about shopping and he seemed kind of off, so I thought I did something wrong. Same thing, right?"

"Perhaps, but I'm not sure."

"I tell ya what, if you ever have a bad feeling about me going somewhere, I'll be happy to stay here in the biggest apartment in the whole world." He stretched out his arms and dug down deep for his thousand-dollar smile.

She put the frame back on the table and pulled Eddie in close. He cleared his throat. "Got an idea to help you—maybe me and Tommy could stay here sometimes so you not so lonely. He's so smart, also a lot bigger than me and he'll take care of you, too. Can I bring him over?"

"No, I don't think so."

"Things go better with Tommy—he's the best! Nobody bothers me when I'm with him, but when I'm on my own, like in the dorms at the Newsboys Lodging House, I get in trouble—they threw me out on my first night. Do you know what Tommy did when that happened?"

"No. What did he do?"

"He left his bed and followed me out into the street. No newsie leaves on a Thursday—that's pork 'n' beans night. He looks out for me, now I'm hopin' I can help him, too."

"I understand, but I'm not so sure about this. I tell you what, I want to give you an invitation to come back for a visit. Either tomorrow for the Schuetzen Day Parade right here in Little Germany or Wednesday for the steamship ride and picnic on Long Island—plenty of hot dogs, fun, and games. You can be my guest. What do you say? Which one do you want to go to?"

"Wow, you really inviting me? I never been on a steamer, but I'm a newspaperman. Can't miss work for a Shitzy Day, though."

"No, not Shitzy! It's the Schuetzen Day Parade, which is part of a larger celebration, Schuetzenfest. A club called the Schuetzen Bund is in charge and their members are the best marksman, so shooting tournaments are a popular part of the day."

"I not so sure . . . the Shitzy parade run by a Shitty Band with shitty shooting contests. Is the music shitty too? This is a whole lot of shitty, Mrs. Heinrich, and what kind of shooting are they gonna be doing? Don't tell me . . ."

Gerda interrupted his play on words with a laugh and an observation. "I think you'll prefer the boat ride and picnic. You ever heard of a paid vacation? I'll give you one of those on Wednesday. How much you make every day?"

"Fifty cents, if I sell out."

"Okay, I'm putting these two quarters right here on my desk and you can come back here with me and collect your vacation pay. What do you say?"

"Sounds like the best day ever." Eddie rushed out of the apartment excited with his news, but he needed to figure out a way to include Tommy. *How could anyone not want him around? Mrs. Heinrich never met him! This is the problem! Easy to fix! The three of us together. What a day!*

Part Two

The Dream
June 13 & 14, 1904

CHAPTER 18

SS Grand Republic

AFTER WAKING UP so early with his vivid dream, Bodee had time to kill so he took a long walk toward Kleindeutschland before heading over to the docks. He noted the German language evident in most storefronts as he walked by the intersection of Houston Street and Avenue D. *This is Little Germany.* The piece of paper with Helmut's address read, 222 Avenue B. *Must be right down this block. I wonder what he'll make of my dream?*

Bodee glanced at his pocket watch—he still had time to spare and continued his leisurely stroll. *222 Avenue B. Helmut and his father must live above their business, Wagner Meats.* Next door was a shoemaker, two doors down, a tailor. The next several shops included a cabinetmaker, baker, another butcher shop, and a beer garden. Kleindeutschland provided everything a German family might need. *With all of this available, why are there so many for-rent signs?* Bodee wondered.

Many of the residents walked the streets at this early hour, but several seemed unwilling to share the sidewalk with Bodee and moved to the side. One young woman passed him, smiled, and offered, "Guten Morgen." Based on the tone, he figured it was a pleasant greeting and tipped his cap. An older man popped out of an adjacent tenement and ushered the woman in another direction.

Bodee came upon a family loading boxes onto a wagon and overheard some of their conversation.

"But, Father, why do we have to move? My friends are here and my school is down the road. St. Mark's is nearby. Why do we have to go, Father?"

"Kleindeutschland is not what it used to be, Gustav. You will be reunited with many of your old friends once we settle uptown in Yorkville—the apartments are larger, the life is better. Whoever you leave behind will probably join us in a matter of months or years. But we've spoken of this before. Time to go."

Another family leaving Little Germany was not an uncommon occurrence. The exodus had been quite dramatic. By some estimates, more than half the population had relocated to Yorkville on the Upper East Side over the last few years.

Well, at least the for-rent signs aren't a mystery. Bodee didn't see any movement through the Wagner's window and assumed he and his father had left for the day. Four men grimaced at him from across the street and disturbed his train of thought. One called out, "Leave now. You have no business here." Given the absence of Helmut's support and protection, waiting in front of the Wagner's door would prove to be a bad move. *No reason to bother Helmut about last night, let me go to work.*

Bodee boarded at 6:45 for his 7:00 a.m. shift. His task for the day—shadow Duane as he went through the duties of a porter.

"You may daydream on the job, but you sure do show up on time!"

"Sorry, Duane. I was thinking about some stuff on Saturday."

"Not a problem for me, but might be for the first mate. So stay clear of him if your mind ever goes on vacation again. All right, you follow me 'round today and I'll show you what to do. The first stop is the lamp room. Right over here."

The two porters walked into a small room down below with no windows. The room contained several portable lamps as well as the entire stock of oil. In addition, cans of varnish, paint, brass polish, and other materials were strewn all over the floor.

Duane entered and lit a lantern in the corner for light, tossing the match on the ground and stomping out the flame with his foot. "We come down here every morning and pick up the oil we need for the upper decks and take a few of the lamps with us. I'll show you where we put them up top."

"Understood. I'll bring the oil."

"The drum is heavy, so I should take it. I think we're going to use you to fit into tight places, but maybe not carry the stuff that weighs more than you do. Okay?"

"Not sure what you're sayin', but I'm fine." Bodee bent at the knees and his legs helped him lift the drum. He was relieved when they decided to stop halfway up the stairs to fill a lantern. They moved on to refill the largest lamp on the main level. Bodee noticed the imprint on the life preservers hanging on the wall, *Passed June 18, 1894.* "Damn, these life jackets go back ten years. Are you sure they still work?"

Duane chuckled. "The inspectors came by beginning of last month—like they do every year—and said they fine."

"Why you laughing?"

"Because the jackets can be fine for ten dollars and fabulous for twenty. I think this was a ten-dollar year."

"So they take bribes, but aren't you worried when you're out at sea?"

"We don't go out so far. Every trip is a couple of hours, tops. If anything ever happened, we'd be back in port in a few minutes and we got an experienced captain who been on these waters for a lot of years."

"He sounds real old," Bodee remarked as a voice came from behind.

"Makes sense, he is real old," Captain Pease joked as he walked by the two men.

"I'm sorry, sir. Didn't mean to say nothing bad." *Why can't I stay out of trouble? I hope I didn't just lose another job.*

"No worries, young man. You must be the new porter, what's your name?"

"My name is Bodee Rivers."

"The fact is, I'm not so young anymore. What do you think of the ship?"

"Best in New York."

"I like your attitude, Bodee. Keep showing him around."

Gilbride appeared as soon as Pease left the area. "I thought I told you not to ask the captain any questions."

"Yes, sir, you did, but he was sayin' hello is all."

"Why are your hellos so long? I don't want to worry about you. Duane, keep an eye on your new friend. Make sure he doesn't talk to Pease anymore."

"Yes, sir."

The first mate walked off to inspect another section of the deck, and the orientation of the new employee continued. "Listen, Knickerbocker has a few ships and they like to do things the same way on all of them. Right now you working with me on the *Republic*, but if you go to another one, everything will be in the same place, done in the same way, and in the same order—we call this the Knickerbocker Way. So you need to pay attention."

"I will. No more daydreaming, I promise."

"Come on, we still got some cleaning up to do before the passengers board. Grab the mop, we need to go up top and make it shine. Everything got to sparkle. We may not be the fanciest anymore and we're far from the newest, but that's how this old girl keeps going, we polish the decks, varnish the wood, and paint until we run out."

Bodee's mind returned to his vision as he thought of the door, which was now in view. He stopped in his tracks and considered the significance of what was about to happen. *Juba told me to go through the door and see if I felt or saw something, but I'm going from the outside to the inside, supposed to be the other way around . . ."*

Duane snapped his fingers. "You promised to stay in the here and now. Did I just lose you? Gilbride pops up out of nowhere, whenever and wherever he wants. Better be careful. See that sign, the *SS Grand Republic*? Right on the door? You figured out what it means yet?" He paused but quickly answered his own question. "SS stands for Shiny Shiny. Yes, that's right. This be the *Shiny Shiny Grand Republic*!" He laughed as he pushed the door open. Bodee hesitated for a moment before passing through, but didn't want to hear another daydreaming comment and proceeded—he felt nothing. *Just a door. No tremendous light. Nothing to fear. I think I made a big deal about nothing.*

"You right, Duane. I think you and I are the king and prince of shine, so we better start moppin'! I'll let you be the king today, but know the prince plans on movin' up! Better watch out!"

"Okay, let's make it shine!"

CHAPTER 19

The Schuetzen Bund Parade

"MAYOR MCCLELLAN, HERE they come. Aren't they impressive?" the aide asked as the mounted trumpeters, who led the procession, entered Union Square Park. A line of kettle drummers followed the blaring, and the combination of the graceful melody and forceful percussion drew the attention of all. Next up were three thousand marksmen dressed in colorful uniforms. The sharpshooters proudly displayed their rifles as they neared the reviewing stand.

"Yes, a stirring sight. Make a note to return next year—the Schuetzen Bund Parade may soon become as grand as St. Patrick's Day."

"Yes, sir. German-American sentiment is on the rise and could be substantial help to you later this year during your presidential run."

McClellan laughed. "Are you implying my presence here today is due to political expediency?"

"I am, sir. Good thinking!"

The two men shared a laugh. A consistent pro-German tide had been building for years. By 1904, many colleges insisted students learn the language and the philosophical treatises of Goethe. People across the country listened to the music of Beethoven, Brahms, Handel, Mozart, and Strauss. Foods like hot dogs and strudel were popular all over the city, but the most important contribution of this community was their wonderful beer.

"Do you think it's too early for a little something to drink?"

"Not for you, sir. What will it be?"

"I'm partial to Schlitz."

"I'll arrange for it, sir, and won't hold it against you."

"You are filled with witty comments today. What won't you hold against me?"

"Well, sir, I thought you would have known."

"What are you talking about?"

"The best beer is Rheingold! That's my favorite!"

The aide noticed Reverend Haas from St. Mark's approaching the seating area as he rose to get the drinks. He turned to his boss. "May I invite him up? He, more than anyone, can swing the local German vote."

"Don't be so obvious with our intentions. You could have just asked if I wanted to say hello—of course I do. Please bring him over."

Helmut Wagner and his father joined Haas as he approached the platform.

"Mayor McClellan, so nice of you to come to this grand event."

"The pleasure is all mine. I understand you're doing some great work over at St. Mark's."

"We do the best we can, Mr. Mayor. I'd also like to introduce two of my parishioners, Helmut Wagner, who is my most active volunteer, and his father, Dieter, one of the top butchers in Little Germany."

"One of the top . . . no, no . . . I am the finest butcher in Kleindeutscheland. Stop by any time, sir, I'll take excellent care of you."

"I'm sure you will. Please enjoy the day."

⇀═◉ ◉═↼

"Tommy, I'm going to go over to Mrs. Heinrich. We need to get her to like you, so you can come with us on the steamship. Walk over after I wave."

Eddie ran toward Gerda Heinrich, who stood on the side of the road with a group of women. He waited for her to finish her conversation.

"Yes, it will be an outstanding day! This year, I have the honor of being in charge of all the preparations. I'm so nervous. I want this to be the best excursion ever!"

"We're so happy you're in charge—it must give someone like you a sense of purpose after everything that happened . . . poor dear."

Gerda lowered her head, but was determined not to let jealous Emily Hausgrotten get to her yet again. "Yes, and maybe you will find some purpose one day as well. I'll thank you to not bring up my misfortune every time you speak to me."

Emily exclaimed, "Well, I never . . ." as she stormed away. Gerda felt a tap on the back, turned, and scooped Eddie up in a hug. "Here he is, ladies! This is the boy from the park." Eddie started waving.

Tommy began a slow walk in their direction, and Gerda's brow tightened. He paused to straighten his shirt and tried to slick back his hair. He called out, "Got to go to work, Eddie. Be seeing you around." Gerda's smile returned.

"But Tommy, you got to come and say hello," Eddie answered.

Gerda pulled him close. "Let him go, he must have things to do. How about a hot dog?"

⊷⊷⊷ ⊷⊷⊷

"Yes, Reverend Haas, everything is perfect for the annual outing. The steamship is confirmed and I helped Gerda as much as I could. As long as it doesn't rain, this will be the best day ever for St. Mark's!"

"I always appreciate your enthusiasm, Helmut, and I realize you worked hard on this, but it doesn't have to be the best day in our history. I'd settle for a pleasant day without any major issues or problems."

Helmut became lost in his thoughts. *If I'm excited, he shoots me down and if I'm pessimistic, he cautions me about being negative. Father spoke to him—he won't admit it, but I know he did. Why would the leader of St. Mark's want to discourage me from pursuing a life in the church? It doesn't make any sense.*

Dieter Wagner tapped his son on the shoulder. "Here they come! What an exciting display of Prussian pride, and can you believe the bürgermeister of New York City is with us today! People think he's Irish because of his name, but he was born in Dresden, so he's one of us and he might be the next president of the United States! What do you think of that?"

"Something to be proud of, but I think he actually is Irish and his family was just visiting Germany when he was born."

"Why do you have to say that? You were born in New York, and you call yourself an American. He was born in Dresden, so why can't he call himself German?"

"Yes, I see your point, Father. Mayor McClellan will be a fine German president!"

Chapter 20

Nellie

Bodee arrived at the agreed-upon location in Tompkins Square fifteen minutes before Nellie and began to unwrap one of the sandwiches he made back at home. She carried the blanket, napkins, and some drinks in a basket.

"Been a long time since I seen you, Bodee Rivers."

"A whole forty-eight hours."

"You find out where Tangiers is yet?"

"Nah, I'm not going to do your job."

"How you figure? You come walkin' up to me slapping yourself in the face, talkin' about Spanish marines, and askin' me about some silly place called Tangiers. How this my job?"

"First of all, I didn't say Spanish marines. Not so sure they exist, and I only hit my head because when you smiled, you flashed the whitest teeth I ever seen in my life. Blinded me, I tell you! I slapped myself to see again!"

"What kind of thing is this to tell a girl? My teeth made you blind? How about, you have the most beautiful smile . . ."

"Yep, you sure do."

"And the most charming personality."

"The best ever."

"So how come you got me complimenting myself? Isn't this supposed to be your job?"

"My job is to find out where those marines are hiding—could be anywhere!

"Watch out! I think they down here!" He scurried to her side and draped the blanket up over both of them and delivered the sweetest kiss on the side of her cheek. He started to uncover their heads, but she pulled him close and whispered, "You went through all this trouble with Spanish marines for that little peck?" The next several kisses traveled slowly from the cheeks to the lips. A gust of wind blew off their covering, and their conversation migrated to other topics.

"Tell me, Mr. Rivers, why should I pick you for my boyfriend? What makes you the one?"

"Well, I can run faster than anyone you'll ever meet."

"So when things get serious, you'll be able to run away real quick?"

"No, my running is for baseball. I'll take you to a game one day."

"What team you on?"

"Not on any team no more. Almost got on one of the best Colored teams around, The Brooklyn Monitors."

"Sorry things didn't work out, but I'm happy I met me a tall, fast, and handsome ball player." Nellie took hold of his bicep. Despite the fact her fingertips almost touched on the underside of his arm, he never felt like a more powerful man.

"Thanks, but I'm not so strong—working on it, though. I got a lot going on, and parts are hard to understand."

"Like what?"

"My dreams."

"What about them?"

"The things I remember from dreams happen."

"Ah, is this your way of saying I'm a dream come true? That's so sweet of you!"

"Funny, but I'm not joking. I get visions every once and a while and Juba understands and she's helping me to sort them out by teaching me how to use my third eye. Crazy, right? I thought so, too, but what she showed me helps. The most important dream involves the ship I'm working on—something is going to happen and I need to find out what."

"Listen, you're tellin' me about this stuff for the first time. I can't say I understand everything, but you better be careful if you're planning to go to your boss and tell him you're afraid of something bad happening because of something you dreamed. He'll think you lost your mind and you'll lose your job. I'm telling you, Bodee Rivers, I'm not dating a man with no job."

"Jobs are no problem for me. I find them easy. Holding on to them, though, is a different story!"

Nellie folded her arms across her chest and glared. "I'm changing the subject because you're not taking me seriously. Tell me about the third eye thing."

"Give me your hand."

"Where you planning on putting it? We already kissed and you better not get fresh with me because I'm already worried about your job—don't make me worry about nothing else!"

"Touch the spot between my two eyes."

"Guess that's okay." She extended the index finger on her right hand while he closed his eyes. "What should I feel?"

"Not sure, but we need to do this the way I learned—Juba showed me this third eye thing while I was kind of awake."

"A daydream?"

"Yeah, except I heard her and she told me what to do to find out more about this thing with the boat. Juba wanted me to think of the waves to calm down and then told me to find the steamship out in the water."

"Don't think I want you swimming on me right now, so let's do something else. How about going backward? Try to relax by thinking of your mother when you little, so you'll remember something pleasant. No need to spoil our day."

"Not so sure about going back. This more about looking forward, but I guess we can try."

"All right, lie down. We'll roll up the tablecloth for a pillow. Tell me when you're ready."

"Ready."

"Think about an early memory—a morning you woke up with everything right in your world. Your mom made you breakfast and you're going out to do something enjoyable for the day."

"Okay. We went to the park a lot. I ran around and played with the other kids."

"Little Bodee is outside running around. Rest . . . smile . . . relax. You're having fun. No one can catch you—you're the fastest of them all! The boys and girls are giggling and enjoying the sunshine. Everyone saying, 'Bodee is the fastest one.'"

He drifted off—the cooling wind complemented the heat from the sun. Five-year-old Bodee was back in Weeksville.

"Bodee, this ain't fair. No one can catch you. Let's play something else. Race you to the swings!"

Bodee won.

"Bet you I can go higher on the swings than you, Bodee Rivers!"

Bodee climbed twice as high as his friend, Marlon, and shouted, "I'll reach the sun!"

Marlon placed his feet down to get off the seat and complained, "You beat me at everything. This not fair! You never let me win! I'm not gonna play with you no more, and I'll tell my grandmother you not playin' fair!"

Bodee screamed, "And I'll tell my grandmother you can't keep up. Grandma Juba, he can't keep up, he can't . . ."

Bodee's mother locked her son in a bear hug from behind. She threw him off the swing to the ground. He scrambled to his feet as the children became silent and stopped playing.

Akua scolded him, "What I tell you about speaking about Juba? She no kin to you or me!"

"Only fooling. I said Grandma Juba . . ." Whack! Akua struck Bodee on the side of his head and her ring dug into his ear.

"Told you don't ever say her name."

"But Juba my grand—" Whack!

"You want more? 'Cause I got plenty!" She formed a fist. Blood trickled down from Bodee's ear. "You think a little bleeding will make a difference? Ain't no matter to me."

The children stopped laughing and ran to their parents. Five-year-old Bodee crawled into a ball in the dirt. Akua stood above him, repeating, "I dare you to say her name again. Go ahead. Try me."

Nellie placed the palm of her hand on the spot between his eyes and stroked his cheek in order to gradually bring him back to the present.

"Bodee, I'm not sure what happened, but this not the right memory. Let's drink something."

"Don't make me go back no more. Need to go forward. Ain't no sense reliving bad things. Sorry if I scared you."

"You don't scare me, but you sure do surprise me an awful lot. We'll stay in 1904, and if you're lucky, one day soon we'll start talking about the future."

He smiled and leaned in for another kiss.

Arlin McFarland and Jimmy McPhee took seats on a bench facing the picnic area in Tompkins Square. He continued his complaining. "I don't think I'll ever learn this singing bullshit, why can't you guys be regular gangsters like everyone else?"

"I like you, Arlin, but you got to stop with all this you sayin' about the Whyos. This is our thing—our secret signals scare the crap out of our enemies. If Shamus finds out you're not letting this go, you're done."

"Fuck McTiernan and fuck the Whyos. One day you and I will take a trip to Chicago and I'll show you how a real gang operates. I led a crew and understand how to get things done."

"Stop talking shit, you're about to dig your grave. I don't like hearing all this. You can't say or even think this kind of thing. Shamus will kill you if you keep this up."

"I'll try and watch what I do for a while, but I'm coming after McTiernan when the time is right. You're with me, or at least I think you are, so there will always be a piece of what I take for you—you'll be a rich man. How does that sound?"

"Fine, but let's be clear, I never said I'm with you. Remember, you only been a Whyo for a few days, so you better slow down because if Shamus gets any idea you're coming after him, you're a dead man. This is dangerous. Do you understand what I'm saying?"

"Yes, you're negotiating. I only offered one slice, but now, they'll be two! Everybody has their price."

"You're not listening to me at all."

"Ah, what are—"

Jimmy interrupted as he pointed. "Looky here, the Darkey who bumped into you at Snake Eyes is having a date with a cute young thing. Do you wanna go and say hello?"

"No, I promised to leave him alone. He's protected somehow, but I didn't say anything about staying away from some Black girl. I'll meet up with you later for the job. Right now, I want to follow the girl to make sure she gets home safe. Least I can do."

CHAPTER 21

A Change of Key

ARLIN MCFARLAND AND two other gang members rushed into the small shipping office and realized their disadvantage in numbers. McFarland quickly smashed two of the larger men with his baseball bat. The first took a shot across the side of his neck and the second man absorbed his first contact in the abdomen, causing him to double over, and then received a crushing blow on his back. The remaining three men backed against the wall and Arlin took charge. "On your knees, all three of ya. Down on the ground."

In the street, Shamus McTiernan and three other Whyos stood back-to-back and waited for their leader to signal the beginning of their part of the operation. Shamus began when Arlin and company crashed through the door. "Okay, fellas, one, two, three, four." The group commenced their rendition of "Finnegan's Wake" in the key of C. A crowd started to form around the talented men, who each trained their eyes in a different direction, looking out either for police or others who might interrupt their activities.

"Tim Finnegan lived in Wattling Street
A gentle Irishman mighty odd
He'd a beautiful brogue so rich and sweet
To rise in the world he carried a hod.

See he'd sort of a tripling way
With love for a liquor poor Tim was born
To help him on with his work each day
He'd a drop of the Craythor every morn'."

Arlin barked, "Where the fuck is the safe?" as he picked up his bat and advanced toward the kneeling men. All three pointed to a closet and one of them blurted, "Ten, twenty-four, thirty-six, twelve—that's the combination, ten, twenty-four, thirty-six, twelve."

"I heard you the first time, but thank you for being so helpful!" Arlin said as he walked over to the closet, dialed the numbers, and took out two stacks of cash. "This is what we're going to do. We'll require this much," he held up a stack, "because it's owed for protection, but I'm taking more to encourage better behavior on your part in the future." He dug back in for another fistful of bills. "We'll be on our way, as soon as—"

"Hold on, let me listen for a second," Jimmy McPhee called out.

One of McTiernan's men spotted two policemen heading their way and stopped singing. He coughed and pointed. Shamus raised his hand and the men shifted to the key of D.

> "One morning Tim was rather full
> His head felt heavy, which made him shake
> Fell from the ladder and broke his skull
> So they carried him home, his corpse to wake.

> Rolled him up in a nice clean sheet
> And laid him upon the bed
> A bottle of whiskey at his feet
> And a gallon of porter at his head."

McTiernan's audience covered their ears when the key shifted—the new tones conflicted with the expectations created by the old. A few scowled and walked away, but those who remained soon began enjoying the song again.

Inside the office, Jimmy confirmed what he thought. "They changed the key, something's wrong. Got to get out of here, through the back."

Arlin tipped his hat to his victims. "Top of the evening to ya," he said as he stuffed McTiernan's money into an envelope and the penalty into his own pocket.

McTiernan's men shifted one last time back to their original key for the last stanza.

"And whack Fol-De-Dah now dance to your partner
Welt the floor, your trotters shake
Wasn't it the truth I told you
Lots of fun at Finnegan's wake."

The remaining audience walked away after the second modification of key. One screamed, "You boys need a little more practice—not saying there's no talent, but some training wouldn't hurt!" The other people in the street laughed and the singers bowed.

McPhee noticed the second shift in key right away. "Must have been a false alarm, they switched back. We can leave through the front."

Arlin asked Jimmy to stay back for a word. "Jimmy, remember what I told you—the penalty was my extra pie, and I promised you two slices. We'll settle up later."

Once the Whyos were all together, the whispers began, "Why-o, Why-o, Why-o, Why-o," in a one-two rhythm. McTiernan anchored the gang both melodically and operationally as its base. The eerie whisper encouraged the final street spectators to go about their business. After a few moments, the volume increased to such a fever pitch that the tone-deaf McFarland joined in without doing much damage. McTiernan brought the war cry to an end with a raise of his hand and the gangsters provided the musical resolution to their evening of crime. They headed toward Snake Eyes to celebrate their successful performance both inside and outside the office.

CHAPTER 22

A Special Kind of Smoke

BODEE WOKE UP in a sweat after experiencing a reoccurrence of his vision. "The light was so hot and the floor . . . hot, too. Need to get up."

Juba interrupted Bodee's half-conscious mumbling. "I'm right here. Are you scared of this heat? You running from the sun?"

"Not sure. I tripped when moving back from the door. I needed the shade, but the thing is most of the upper level is open—not sure where the shade comes from. People are singing and dancing. Don't think anyone's afraid."

"This dream is starting to worry me, but as long as you don't sense danger, we can wait 'til later. Are you sure about this?"

"I think so."

"Not such a definite answer. You sensed danger on the small boat, right?"

"Yes, but I'm not sure. Can't say I felt safe."

"All right, I think we spoke about this enough. You go on to work, but when you're by the door, if something ain't right, like the barbershop sign the other day, you got to move away. Are we clear?"

"Yes, ma'am."

⊷▩ ▧⊷

"All right, Bodee, today is a short day and you'll shadow me one last time. Let's start. Where do we go first?"

"The lamp room."

"Right, lead the way."

The men headed down the stairs and tried to open the door, but it became stuck at the halfway point. "Push, Bodee. Sometimes things shift inside the room and block the door. Put your back into it—can't damage nothing. Other than the lamps, we mostly have different kinds of paint and supplies down here."

He pushed hard and the door opened, but a can of varnish, which had blocked the door, tipped over, spilling a fair amount on the floor. Duane took charge. "Use one of those rags from the corner to clean up. Doesn't need to be perfect—this only the lamp room, no guests in here."

Duane struck a match to light one of the lamps and tossed it on the floor. Bodee ran to the spot and stomped on the match. "We got a bad spill, you got to be careful."

"I been tossing matches on this floor every day for a long time. You think this is the first varnish ever done spilt down here? You worry too much. Grab the oil, and let's head on upstairs."

Bodee bent his legs to pick up the heavy drum and noticed how much easier it was than just a few days earlier. *This work is what I needed to be stronger!* He carried the drum the entire distance without taking a break.

"I think you showing off! I thought for sure you'd stop along the way. You getting the hang of this."

Duane slipped on a pool of spilled oil as they arrived at the upper level. "We gonna need to spray these floorboards down before we try to clean them. Go run the hose from the pump on the pier."

"Why? You got hose right here on the wall next to the water connection. Let's hook them up. No need to go on down to the dock."

"Ain't been no water pressure in those pipes for years, and this hose too old to hold water nohow. We need to run it from down below, go on."

"Did the inspectors check out the hose as well as they checked the life jackets?"

"Yeah, and they said it fine."

"Ten dollars, fine?"

"You're learning fast!"

⊷═◑ ◐═⊷

By 9:00 a.m., Captain Pease was in position at the entrance to the gangway and he greeted passengers from different tour groups who pooled resources for the short three-hour excursion around the southern end of Manhattan. Bodee didn't understand all of the languages being spoken, but the first mate, Gilbride, said some were French and the rest British.

A teenage boy ran up and pointed. "Mister, I see smoke—must be a fire."

Bodee was surprised at how slowly Pease turned to investigate the boy's claim. "Thank you for telling me, but I want you to think twice about saying the words smoke and fire, because if people become frightened, we will have a problem. Did you ever smell smoke before in your life?"

"Yes, sir, when my daddy put out a fire in my kitchen."

"Okay, come with me." He walked the boy over to the location of the smoke and they both stood in the middle of it. "Does this smell like smoke?"

"No, sir, it does not."

"Did you ever watch the teakettle boil on your stove?"

"Yes, sir."

"What comes out of the spout?"

"Steam, sir."

"What type of ship is this?"

"A steamship, sir . . . oh, sorry. I guess we'll see lots of this kind of *smoke* today!"

The people who gathered after hearing the boy's screams enjoyed the captain's explanation and offered a round of applause.

A middle-aged gentleman in a distinctive English accent added, "Jolly good elucidation, Captain, and what a wonderful vessel—everything is tip-top."

"We work hard to keep the old lady in the best possible shape. Thanks for the compliment," the caption said, as he turned and winked at his two hard-working crew members. The king and prince of shine smiled in return.

"Duane, you ever heard anyone talk like those British folks? Is this what English is supposed to sound like? They must think we speak real funny."

"No, they the funny ones." Duane straightened his back and did his best to imitate the delivery of *everything is tip-top*, in his own version of an English accent. The two porters shared a laugh as they continued directing their ongoing efforts throughout the day toward picking up spills, dumping garbage, and spending every spare minute polishing anything and everything they came across. The short trip came to an end at about lunchtime.

"I think you almost ready to be on your own. Tomorrow, I got the day off, but a big German group is coming on board our sister ship. Gilbride loaned you to them for the day and says you need to be on time. Can you read?"

"Sure do."

"Okay, take this paper with the address. Remember, Mr. Daydreamer—don't be late. The steamer is exactly like this one 'cept it newer. Ask for the head porter—his name is Walter."

"You ever work with him before?"

"Yeah, he the one who trained me, but I got to warn you, he's a little tougher than I am. Do what he says and you'll be fine, but sometimes he's hard to get along with. Don't matter if you like him—he's the head porter, so you got to do what he says. Meet him in the lamp room at six thirty in the morning. Things won't go well with him if you start out bad, so no daydreaming on your way to work. Got it?"

"Sure thing, Duane."

CHAPTER 23

Wagner Meats

"YES, FATHER. I understand we must arrive early to make sure we are ready for the day."

"Helmut, I want you and I to work the front, father and son together." He smiled. "Remember, be polite and friendly, but we must keep the line moving, especially before lunch, around eleven a.m."

"Yes, the front is better. Gustav tried to help me in the back the last time I worked, but I can't make those cuts like him."

"That's because you don't put in enough hours to become an expert—you're only here a day or two each week and you'll never learn the business at this pace. Remember, I'm not going to work forever. Oh, hold on, I left my daily list in my bedroom. I'll be right back."

Helmut turned to the portrait of his mother hanging in front of him and whispered, "Mother, I discussed this with him so many times, but he acts like we never did. I respect the business and all it did for us, but it is not for me. Wish me luck today, Mother. Here he is now."

"Son, are you ready for the final inspection?"

"I sure am."

Father and son stood side to side in the full-length mirror. They always started with the shoes. Both men bent and nodded as they approved the high shine and moved upward. Once their ties and hair received slight adjustments, they covered their clothing with freshly washed and pressed white smocks. Helmut turned to his father. "Let's sell some meat, old Mr. Wagner."

"Let's keep the line moving, young Mr. Wagner."

Father and son smiled as they descended the stairs.

"Good morning, Gustav. How long have you been here?" Helmut asked his cousin.

"Guten Morgen. About an hour or so, today will be a busy day. The displays needed to be organized. Are you going to be out front?"

"Yes, but don't worry." Helmut smirked. "I'm much more suited to *this* kind of work."

"Okay. I'll stay out here as long as possible to help you, but I must be in the back in the afternoon to supervise the deliveries. Do you think you'll be able to manage?"

"Thanks for looking out for me and, yes, I'll be fine. Many of our customers will likely ask me questions about tomorrow's excursion, so being out front will . . ."

Dieter Wagner returned to the front. "Remember, today is about business, not church, so unless the discussions are about supplies for the trip, let's concentrate on the shop."

"I understand, Father. Let me open the door for Mrs. Scherber." He walked toward the door, but struggled with the lock. Gustav came over. "Remember, you need to jiggle the handle and then push down."

"Yeah, I forgot. Sorry."

Mrs. Scherber headed directly to Helmut. "I so enjoyed the picnic on Saturday, but the little boy made me sad at the end."

"Yes, I agree. We all loved his little game with the hot dogs. I said a prayer for him at services on Sunday."

Dieter added, "Speaking of hot dogs, what would you like today?"

"One pound of your best veal."

"Excellent. Helmut, why don't you help her?"

Mrs. Scherber cleared her throat. "Mr. Wagner, would it be okay if Gustav prepared my order? Your son is so helpful at St. Mark's, but at the butcher, I do like how your nephew takes care of me."

Dieter nodded and Mrs. Scherber pulled Helmut into the corner of the store to resume their discussion. Over the next few minutes, several other parishioners came in and joined in the conversation. Gustav walked over and did his best to take their orders.

Dieter asked Helmut to meet him in the back for a chat. "You can't talk so much with everyone. Not only are you asking how people are, you are also giving them advice about their children and getting into all kinds of topics other than their purchases. This is a business. This is our business. This isn't St. Mark's."

"I'm sorry, Father. Less talk and more sales, but you must admit, everyone is leaving with a smile."

"It is always so hard to be mad at you! You and your cousin do work well together, and you are right, everybody is happy, but our rush is coming up, so let's focus on business."

"Father, I think it is *you* and Gustav who are the good team. Actually, he is impressive on his own. Take a peek." The two men walked to the window overlooking the counter. Gustav had everything under control. "I'm not the only one who can make them smile."

>─═◉ ◉═─<

Dieter reflected on his day as he climbed the stairs. He stopped by the painting of his deceased wife, Emily, and reported on his day. "I hoped our son would finally show interest in the business today. He is such a fine man, but if we must have one area of disagreement, why must it be this? My dear, Emily, what are we going to do?" Dieter remembered all of their chats as a young couple about the future and wished he'd spent more time living in the present while she was alive. Her eyes were always the key and he studied them as he waited for an answer. After some time, he touched the edge of the frame, nodded, and walked away.

Chapter 24

That Ain't No Marcus

"Bodee, I'm so happy you found yourself a nice girl. I like her name, Nellie. Sounds real friendly, but don't bring her over yet because I don't want her being frightened of the neighborhood. We'll figure out some other way for me to meet her."

"You'll like her, she's special."

"I'm sure I will, but you got a lot going on right now—may not be the best time for a romance. You still don't understand everything you need to about me and Akua, so we're expecting a visitor in a few minutes who'll explain some more. We'll talk at the kitchen table, not downstairs, because he more like family."

"Family? I thought it only the three of us?"

"His name is Marcus and he'll come upstairs on his own. Sit at the table."

Bodee heard footsteps coming up the staircase.

Juba set three cups on the table and said, "Come join us over here."

Bodee remarked, "That ain't no Marcus. It's Blood."

"You think my parents named me Blood? What kind of crazy name is that for a child?"

"Is your name really Marcus?"

"Yes."

Juba clarified, "Bodee, I never told this to you proper, so I decided to tell you when we all together. Akua never mentioned him?"

"No, ma'am, she didn't. Only spoke about you, and not so much."

"Not surprising. Akua angry with both of us when she left Minetta. Something bad happened, but first I want to tell you about Marcus."

Bodee took a sip of his tea. "Go ahead."

"I told you how we took a boat up the Mississippi and one of the slaves hid us?"

"Yeah."

"Well, he helped us because I promised to take his fifteen-year-old boy, Marcus, to freedom. He stayed with us in the little room. In Ohio, we snuck off the ship. Marcus said goodbye to his dad and we all went to New York."

"I never saw my father again, and lived in this apartment with your grandma and Akua. She like a little sister to me."

Bodee directed his question to Marcus. "Where did the whole Blood thing come from?"

Marcus lowered his head, and Juba answered. "Marcus was a fierce child who could scare grown men with his glare. When we got the chance to live here, your mother was about seventeen years old. I wasn't sure we could stay because it so rough, but Marcus got us respect."

Juba stopped to take a breath. "He did bad things to make his reputation. I found a way to create some order in the Bend, but to do that I needed an enforcer, and that's Marcus. People scared of him because he didn't take shit and they afraid of me because they think I'm a mambo." Juba waved her hands over her head and snapped her fingers. "How you like my black magic?"

"Not so much."

"After a couple of years, we started running things. Been in charge ever since as Madame Juba and Blood. I'm the brains and he's the brawn. He kind of an uncle to you."

"So, Blood, I mean, Marcus, you're not a criminal?"

"Not saying that at all, I ain't got an honest bone in my body." Juba flashed a stare and Marcus reconsidered his answer. "I do criminal things, but I follow Juba's rules about who we steal from, and I make others on the block do the same. Whenever they don't, I make an example of them."

"So you and my grandma make the law around here?"

"No reason to call it law—ain't nothing legal about what we do—call it a code, written by Juba and enforced by me. Not much of a problem with the Black folks, but I won't kid you by sayin' the Irish gangs don't test me. The mess you started with the new guy in the Whyos could be a problem—don't think he's forgetting. I know you ain't going back to Snake Eyes no more, but I think he may come looking for you."

"I'll be careful, but I'll try to stay out of sight and out of the way. I got a summer job on a steamship, so I shouldn't be around so much."

"All right, but I'll keep an eye on you because you'll need some looking after."

"So, do I call you Uncle Marcus?"

"No. Call me Blood, like always."

"So what bad thing happened between my mother and the two of you?"

Juba held her finger up and Blood understood she wanted to respond. "I wish your mama done told you something, because you'll hear one side from me and there are two sides to everything. This part not easy to tell. What Akua tell you about your daddy?"

"She said he died before I born and she missed him."

"Those two things are true, but there's a lot more to his story. Your daddy's name was Antuan, but they called him Slice, and he was one of the street folks here in Minetta. Never was shy about telling everyone he wanted to replace Blood as boss. Your mother was sweet on him, and I warned her about trouble if she tried to get close, but she didn't listen. He got your mama liquored up one night, beat her up some, had his way with her, and she got pregnant with you. Akua couldn't see straight with him and thought having his baby would make him want to start a family, but he didn't give a damn about her or anyone else. He crossed the line with Blood by attacking his stepsister, who said she not attacked, but her bloody lip and bruises told a different story. Blood needed to act."

"What do you mean, act? What did you do to my father?"

"I killed him."

"You murdered my father!"

"His rape of your mama was him coming after me for control. The way I figured—him or me and only one solution—Slice needed to die. Not gonna lie, what I did was brutal and public. I'm telling you direct because you'll hear this from someone else. He came after everything connected to me and had to go."

"What kind of uncle does something like that?"

"The kind that takes care of what need to be done. If I could go back in time, I'd do the same thing. Your daddy was as low as anyone I ever met."

Bodee jumped up and ran toward the stairs, but Blood grabbed him by the belt. "Sit down. I'm not letting you run off until you calm down and understand. You needed the truth, and while you may hate me now, this is what happened and we all been dealing with this for the last twenty years."

"Jesus, you told me in one sentence—you're my uncle and then in the next—you killed my father. What kind of family is this? This ain't normal. I got to think."

"You think all you want, but remember, he raped your mama, and she blind when it came to him. He messed with all the girls and believe me, he didn't plan on being any kind of daddy to you. I had no choice, but Akua didn't see things that way."

Juba added, "After we buried Antuan, your mother wouldn't look at us. Said she had enough of the violence and my black magic, and up and left. You need to understand, though, I did try to visit you, but Akua always turned me away."

Bodee had to get out of the apartment to think and Blood stepped out of his way. He turned and stared intently at his grandmother and his uncle. Both displayed an unbending clarity of mind—twenty years later, they still believed they did the right thing. *How could killing my father be the only solution? Who are these people that I call family? Maybe my mother was right to walk away.*

CHAPTER 25

Going for A Run

HOW COULD HE kill my father? How could Juba approve? Why didn't my mom ever tell me? Got to clear my head. Let me start with a few laps around the park, Bodee thought as he began his run.

His long effortless strides quickly made him the source of attention of a group of young men who were also planning to stretch their legs. Two of them raced to catch him, but Bodee accelerated and his challengers ended their pursuit. Bodee continued at this quicker pace and experienced the high he often did at the peak of exercise. The spot between his two eyes became hot as a daydream began.

He found himself in a variation of Juba's apartment—different furniture, a new color paint on the walls, and toys strewn all over the floor. The salt and pepper shakers, however, were both in their holders on the table. Nellie walked out of the bedroom and was followed by a little boy, perhaps seven, who jumped into Bodee's arms. "Daddy, you promised to play with me today, and now you're going to work. I hate work."

Nellie interjected. "Leave your father be. If he don't go to work, we won't have no money to buy more food."

"No matter, we eat too much."

"No money for clothes, either."

"It summer, we don't need no clothes." He began stripping off his shirt as he giggled.

"All right, Marcus, if your father don't go to work, they'll be no more money for toys!"

"Have a nice day at work, Daddy!" Everyone laughed as he put his shirt back on and sat at the table for breakfast.

Bodee continued his run throughout his daydream and had enough control over his body to navigate the curves and straightaways while devoting the most attention to his third eye. At the moment Nellie called their son Marcus, he lost concentration and ran straight into a low fence and fell forward. He quickly sat up to take stock of his physical condition, as well as make sense of his vision.

The two boys who tried to catch him came onto the scene. "You okay, mister? Didn't you see the fence? Boy, were you flying!"

"Yeah, I'm okay. Thanks for asking."

"You must be a professional baseball player."

"Why you say that?"

"I'm a fan. I like the Brooklyn Monitors and I saw your shoes."

"Tried to be, but they didn't take me."

"You should try again. Will you give us your autograph? This way when you're famous, we can say we met you."

The other boy pulled a pencil and a scrap of paper from his pocket. "My name is Johnny."

"My name is George."

Bodee wrote the same thing to both boys: *To Johnny & George, my first fans and the only people who ever beat me in a race!*

The boys walked away laughing as they read their notes, leaving Bodee alone with his thoughts. *So, Nellie will be my wife and our boy will be named after Marcus. This means I'll not only forgive him, but honor him. I do trust Juba and Marcus and my father sounds like he was as bad as bad can be. It's twenty years later . . . I think we all got to move on.*

CHAPTER 26

Arlin and Nellie

"ARLIN, I TOLD you the 'Whyos way' worked—the first key change signaled something was wrong and the second, not to worry," Jimmy McPhee offered.

"Big fucking deal. Instead of the sissy singing, the sound of a whistle or a knock on the door might have been our signals. How about how well the 'Chicago way' worked on the inside. My first snatch got what we came for." Arlin took out the oversized envelope stuffed with cash, "And my second grab, a little extra for us. Remember, you get two slices of the pie."

"I told you about this—you can't make a move on Shamus McTiernan. He'll kill you."

"I'll kick his little girly ass and I'll only give respect to the person above him in the Whyos. I know how these things work—all I need to do is make the case that I'll run things better, and if the higher-ups see what I can do, I'll be the next leader. This is what they call ambition. Stay with me and you'll go all the way to the top!"

"Jesus, you been a Whyo for three days, slow down."

"No reason to go any slower than the rest of the gang because as far as I can tell, you guys are crawling. We'll pick up the pace and make some money, so shut up with your warnings and take your cut." McFarland handed McPhee a stack of bills. "Here you go, welcome to the team. You never asked me why I recruited you first? Aren't you interested?"

"Okay, tell me why I was first."

"Ambition is tricky; you got to figure out who's ripe for the taking, like McTiernan. Then, you should also keep an eye on the people below you because they might also be ambitious. My take on you, Jimmy, is that you'll be a loyal number two and watch my back. Am I right? Will you watch my back?"

"In your first few days as a Whyo, you figured out your boss is ready to be taken down and I could be a loyal number two, so who am I to disagree with such a smart person? Let's go for a drink later after our last job to celebrate."

"You're finally getting into the right spirit! One last thing—I need you to cover for me for a while tonight because I'm planning a little fun with the Darkey's girl."

"No worries for the first job, but we'll need your muscle for the last collection of the night because we got to go in strong. Make sure you can meet us at the spot by eight."

⊶⊷

"Yes, Mother, Bodee is his name. We met in the park and he is the nicest boy. He grew up in Brooklyn, but moved into New York when his mom died a while ago and lives with his Grandma Juba. He'll be working during the summer on a steamship. The interesting thing is that he used to be a top baseball player. Almost got on one of the Negro League teams, and I think . . . he the one."

"He sounds nice, Nellie, but you only went out with him a couple of times. Slow down with the 'he the one' talk. Too soon. Remember the last boy? Didn't you tell me the same thing after your second date with him?"

"Don't talk about boys from the past! Bodee different. You'll see. He real fast too. He can run like the wind!"

"You seen him run? Is this why you always meeting outdoors?"

"Of course not, but he told me no one can run faster than him."

"Tellin' something and it being true are two different things. I thought I taught you this a long time ago. Boys will tell you all of the good things and none of the bad, and remember, you want to get hitched, but he might just want to get into your knickers, so you be careful."

"He not like that, but he did say some odd things. Didn't understand what he meant, but we didn't have a chance to talk about it too much."

"What he say?"

"Well, he explained about how sometimes the things he sees in his dreams actually come true."

"This boy is crazy! What kind of thing is that to say? What he plannin' to tell you? He had a dream last night about you pulling your skirt up over your head, so you might as well do it?"

"You make everything about people trying to pull my skirt up! The world ain't focused on my clothes, Mama. Anyway, I never pulled it up, not even once. Stop with all this nonsense."

"Don't you sass me, Nellie Washington! I'm lookin' out for you. I know you're a good girl, but I'm just so worried these boys are saying things to trick you. Best thing would be to bring me on your dates—I could sit a few feet away and come over every once and a while and tell you what to do? Great idea, right?"

Mother and daughter laughed. "What a fool idea! I'll never find a husband with you coming along everywhere I go!"

"What other unusual things he tell you?"

"He also said something about not having any power, like muscles or something else. He real thin."

"All right, wait on going out for the milk. If you plan on marrying a bony boy, you'll need to learn how to cook. Got to fatten him up some."

"Now you talkin'! What we making?"

⊷▦ ▦⊶

This damn girl may be in for the night. Still cooking—walking back and forth past the window. Might have to go up there and grab her—already seven thirty. There she goes again with another fucking pan! Arlin McFarland sat on a crate in an alley, watching Nellie Washington's apartment. He knew he couldn't miss the late collection. A show of force was needed and, after only three days on the job, he was the muscle.

"Okay, Nellie. I think you done real well with your cooking lesson and you'll have no problem fattening up that new boyfriend of yours. Why don't you go around the corner for the milk? I'll set the table."

"Sure, Mama. Be right back."

Nellie's path to the corner store took her in front of the spot where the Irish gangster lay in wait. He glanced at his pocket watch as she left her building—7:45.

I'll need at least ten minutes' travel time to the meeting place with the crew. What can I do in five minutes?

A newsie positioned a few feet away cried, "Extra, extra, read all about it, marines in Tangeerie." Nellie thought the young boy meant Tangiers and wanted to pick up the paper to show her boyfriend their favorite place still dominated the headlines. She had just paid for the paper when McFarland grabbed her by the back of her hair and her belt and dragged her inside the alley. The newsie noted the determined look on Arlin's face and left to find another location to hawk his papers.

Nellie screamed, "Help! Help! Help!" McFarland slapped her across the face and she fell to the ground.

"If you're going to keep screaming, the next shot won't be a slap; it will be a punch, and I got to tell ya, you can't afford me rearranging your face. You're already not so much of a looker. You seemed much prettier from a distance, Nellie Washington."

"How you know my name? Who are you? What you want with me?"

"You're not the one asking the questions, but don't worry, you'll understand by the time we're done. First, let me have a peek." He ripped her dress and undergarments down from the collar. "Put your hands down by your sides."

Two passersby, middle-aged White men, rushed to the location of the screams. Arlin turned and took out his switchblade. Nellie raised her hands to cover herself. "No reason for the two of you to be involved—nothing but a Black whore who needs to be disciplined. None of your business, go on."

The two men ran off when Arlin took a step in their direction. He checked again. 7:48.

"Now, where were we? Oh, yes, hands to your side without a punch to the face, or hands to the side after I make you a little uglier? What do you prefer?"

She put her hands down again and he put his knife away. McFarland reached out with both hands. "Let's see what we got here." She flinched and moved back, deeper into the alley.

"Not bad, I see what your boyfriend, Bodee Rivers, sees in you."

"How you know who my boyfriend is?"

"There you go with another question. I'm running short on time, so I'll make my point." He moved toward her and she backed up into the alley.

"You're not so smart, are you? I don't think you understand the further inside you go, the more trouble you're in. Oh, you like what you see? Is that it, Nellie Washington? Is this the first time a real man, not a skinny little Darkey, copped a feel?"

Arlin paused to chuckle at his commentary and glanced at his timepiece. 7:49. "No, no, I'm not going to fuck you now, but I will, and I won't be gentle. You'll remember me for many years to come. I want you to know this is happening because of your stupid-as-shit boyfriend. We'll have him watch, what do you think?"

Things had gone too far and despite his promise of not raping her at that moment, nothing about the encounter seemed to be under control. Nellie decided to fight and screamed, "Help! Help! Help!" He didn't move toward her again, but instead headed out, it was 7:50. "Until we meet again. Please tell Mr. Rivers: Arlin McFarland sends his regards. Top of the evening to ya."

⊰━⊙ ⊙━⊱

"Mama, it was terrible. A real big White man pulled me off the street downstairs. Looked like one of them gangsters—scariest man I ever seen. People heard me scream, but they didn't help. The newsie saw him take me and two men came into the alley—none of them did anything. Either they afraid or didn't care. I never been so scared in my life."

"Before you tell me the middle, tell me the end. Did the man rape you?"

"No, but he promised to come back and do it. He only touched my breasts and said he was doing all of this because of Bodee."

"You done got yourself involved with someone doing bad stuff. Anyone who got dealings with gangsters can't be good. We'll talk about how you gettin' away from this boy later, but right now he got to be told what happened so he can help protect you. As far as I'm concerned, you ain't leaving this apartment 'til this is over."

"Okay, but he's not bad. Can't understand this."

"You think all boys are caring. I wish the world was as half as sweet as you see it, my baby, but it ain't. You told me you know where he lives?"

"Yes, his block is the roughest in the city and he gave me the address so I'd have it, but told me never to go down there."

"I'll take this here rolling pin with me and I'll hit anyone who gets in my way. Let them try and attack me. The thing is, tellin' you it the roughest area probably a lie like all those other things he's been saying. I'm half expecting I'll knock on this door and find out he a married man. What his grandma's name again?"

"They call her Madame Juba in the neighborhood."

"My God, how you fall for all of this? Madame Juba and Bodee Rivers—what kind of names are these? You done picked another real winner this time, but we'll know for sure after your mother is through dealing with the both of them. You stay in this apartment and don't go out for any reason."

Chapter 27

Uncle Marcus

Mabel Washington stopped at the corner of Sixth Avenue and Minetta Lane and studied the stretch of road she needed to navigate. *At least he didn't lie about the neighborhood.* She compared the address to the number on the first building. *The place I want must be halfway down the street. Could be safer if I come up from the other end.*

About ten minutes later, she assessed her safety from the bottom of Minetta and moved forward, but stopped when she heard a scuffle and the sound of metal on metal. Mabel prided herself on her survival instincts and took her baking pin out while rolling up the sleeves of her long dress. *Got to get in the right frame of mind.* She thought back to her anger on the day her husband left for parts unknown and she hurled her two hundred-pound body into the Bend.

"You better all stay the hell away from me, or you'll regret it. I understand what kind of place this is and you're not getting nothing from me—you want to try? Test me, I dare you!" She stopped about every twenty feet, made her speech, and swung her kitchen equipment a few times for effect. Once in the vicinity of the address, she became more specific. "Looking for Madame Juba and Bodee Rivers—either one of them . . ." Blood came onto the scene.

"Put that damn thing down before you hurt somebody. What you want with them?"

"You better just stay where you are. No one will have their way with me!"

The men behind Blood laughed and one mumbled, "No one wants to have their way with you." Blood put his hand up and the comments stopped. "I'm not going to keep repeating myself. Tell me what you want with the two of them, and put that pin down! No one will harm you here. They'll do what I say. My name Blood."

Mabel thought, *Blood, Juba, Bodee—crazy names. What the hell did my daughter get herself into?* "All right, Mr. Blood."

"No, not Mr. Blood, just Blood. That my first and last name, and only name I need."

"Okay, Bodee is dating my girl, Nellie, and he done got her in some trouble and I need to speak to both him and his grandma."

"He right up here with me," Juba called out from her second-story window. "Bring her on up."

Mabel spotted a business card on the table with the inscription *Madame Juba* as she entered the parlor and headed for the back staircase. Up to that moment, no one she'd encountered made her feel any better about her daughter's poor choice in men—then she met Bodee.

"Mrs. Washington, I'm Bodee Rivers. Didn't want to meet you like this, but still nice to make your acquaintance." He extended his hand and they exchanged a cordial shake. "This here my grandma." She breathed a sigh of relief. *I can tell—he is a good boy.*

The two women shook hands, but Juba prolonged and intensified the greeting by using both of her hands for the firmest possible embrace. Juba smiled and Mabel relaxed ever so slightly.

"I came over here because Nellie got attacked tonight in an alley and the man who did it said Bodee was the reason. She's okay—he ripped her clothes and said he didn't have time to do everything he wanted, but threatened to come back—his name is Arlin McFarland."

Blood commented first. "I knew he didn't let this go—he's new with the Whyos and doesn't understand how things work around here. He's trying to make a name for himself and thinks he's being smart because his boss told him to leave Bodee alone, so he's comin' after his girl."

"Are you sure she's okay, Mrs. Washington?" Bodee asked.

"Yeah, she okay, but I'm not letting her out of the apartment until this is over, and why a boy like you mixed up with people like this man who attacked my daughter?"

"I bumped into this man and knocked him backward into a lamppost. He got embarrassed and I done apologized, but he not satisfied. Hard to believe he knew about your daughter, and the fact he came after her is crazy. I'll make this right. Let me go and stay with her and I'll make sure she's okay."

"You do seem like such a nice boy, but this man ain't that way, so we'll need more of a plan than you comin' over for a visit for my child to be safe."

Blood jumped in. "The boy may be polite and nice, but me, not so much. I'll be with him, and we'll fix this—all we need is some time."

Mabel was confused. "You don't want me to call you Mr. Blood because you say the one word is all you need, but how can I trust a man with one word for a name? How are you connected to Juba and Bodee?"

Bodee clarified, "He's my Uncle Marcus, but he don't like using his real name."

"Okay, so you family. Now, I understand." Mabel said.

Juba walked toward the kettle on her stove. "Let's you and I sip some tea while Bodee and Marcus figure this out. We can sit here at the kitchen table like two old friends."

"Fine, but I can't stay too long because I need to go back home soon—worried about my girl."

"We understand," Blood said. "We'll come back in a little while with our plan."

Strength and Power

"I DIDN'T THINK I wanted you to call me Uncle Marcus, but I got to say the name sounds nice. We gonna be okay?"

"Yeah, I decided to think more on why you did what you did and how you been by Juba's side all these years. Never met my father, and I'm starting to think things worked out for the best."

"Happy you saying this, but you came around quick in sorting all this stuff out. Sometimes you give up too soon. Are you sure that you're ready to forgive me for what I done to your daddy?"

"Yeah, I am. My family only you and Grandma."

"Okay, so this not an example of you giving up too soon, because if I'm gonna help you with Nellie, I need to know she's someone you're gonna work hard to help. Ain't no giving up with this kind of thing."

"I only know her for a few days, but she's the one for me and this whole mess she's in is because of me. So, for both reasons I'm helping her, even if I have to do it on my own."

"Glad you're willin' to stand your ground for your girl, but remember, you got family. Your Uncle Marcus will help you." He paused for moment. "I do like my new name!"

Bodee smiled.

"All right, we got two ways to go. The first way is the best, because we won't need to lift a hand against Arlin McFarland, but if it fails, the second thing is to step in so nothing happens to your girl. Let's hope the first way works because stepping in will be messy—we going against one mean Irishman, and we not doing whatever we doing in the Bend. Can you fight?"

"Never done it so much."

"What you mean?"

"I never fought so much."

"So you been leading a charmed life? No one ever go against you, try to take nothing of yours, or make a joke about you? You one blessed Black man!"

"No, all those things happen to me all the time. I pick and choose my battles."

"This won't work if you don't tell me the truth. You say you 'pick and choose,' and I think you never found a battle important enough to take on, and this worries me. So I'll ask you one last time. Are you running away from this here thing or are you planning on taking care of your girl?"

"I'm going to stand my ground for Nellie. This will help me work on my *ti bon ange*."

"Ah, Juba been schooling you on your Voudou. You right, we'll work on your *ti bon ange*. Let's start out with the basics about fighting. You ever go to a boxing match?"

"No. Never did."

"Damn, you sure not makin' this easy! Let's imagine you got a heavyweight weighing two hundred and twenty-five pounds, six feet tall with a barrel chest and a fat stomach. He going against a hundred and fifty-pound man who is five feet seven inches, in top shape, and real fast. Let's also say they about the same age."

"Okay."

"What if the little fella goes toe-to-toe with the two hundred and twenty-five pounder?"

"He won't last long—the heavier man will be too much for him and he won't be able to hit hard enough."

"Now you're thinking. So the little guy got to dart in and out taking little shots and shouldn't try to mix things up until the big man is all tuckered out. Understand?"

"Yeah, I do."

"Same think true with age. I'll give you an example—if you put two fighters in the ring who the same size and weight, but one forty and the other twenty-years-old. The young man should stay out of the way for a while and the old guy should try to do some early damage."

"Makes sense, but what does this have to do with me?"

"Well, as far as I can tell, you a real young man with a lot of speed. So you got to use your quickness and remember if you ever go against an experienced fighter like me or McFarland, you never go straight at him. I'll be with you and we'll do this together."

"I appreciate the advice and help, but I wish I was strong like you."

"You say, 'I wish I was strong like you,' and I hear, 'I'm weak and this'll never change.' This is how you think, Bodee, and this'll be the end of you. Young men don't understand body strength and power not the same things. Most people who grew up like me with lots of muscle go against someone with more at some point and things go the wrong way. Years ago, I wasn't so careful, but I had luck on my side. Now I understand real power."

"Not sure what you mean, but shouldn't we be talking about how we'll get the Irishman?"

"This is the thing. It's not about us getting anybody, it's about us getting what we want. I'll teach you something I learned over the years. Are you ready?"

"Yes, Uncle Marcus."

"You really workin' the name, aren't you?"

"A little bit." Bodee chuckled.

"All right. Am I a big man? Am I a young man?"

"You kind of large, but not so young."

"Fair enough, but when you compare me to the others on Minetta Lane, is anyone larger or younger than me?"

"Some bigger, and most younger."

"So if power about muscle and youth, why am I running shit in the Bend?"

"They scared to go against you."

"Yup, I did a few things a long time ago—could've gone either way, but I was lucky, and people been afraid of me ever since. Lately, I don't raise my hands much at all—when someone needs to be taught a lesson, others step in for me, unless it personal. The longer I been in charge, the more I solve problems with my brain than with my body. You understand?"

"Yeah, I do, but people been calling me a string bean my whole life."

"Juba told me about the whole 'all speed, no power thing.' In real life, power comes more from your brains and how you use the people around you. We got to go visit the man who runs the Whyo crew to try our first way of handling this situation. Hopefully, this will fix things, but if not, we'll figure something else out. No matter what—we will protect Nellie, and this might or might not mean getting Arlin McFarland. Don't be confused about what we trying to do. This all about protectin', not gettin'.'"

"I understand. You make sense."

⋆⊱━◈ ◈━⊰⋆

"Blood, I don't like this. He had his scuffle in here a few days ago and Juba don't want him in here at night. The girls are working the room and I got all my regulars inside, including a few of the Whyos. McTiernan himself is at the bar."

"We'll leave as soon as we done. We'll take a table in the back. Tell Shamus I need a word."

"Okay, but get the kid out of here as soon as you can."

"Will do."

McTiernan placed his empty tumbler in front of him and crossed his arms across his chest. Silvy walked over and provided a refill, but waited for him to finish his conversation before delivering Blood's message. The Whyos leader smiled and turned his attention back to the blathering little man. "Get to the point. Yes, we can help you, but what the fuck do you want? Stop the bullshit, we come here to relax. McFadden, give him the menu."

John McFadden, who often accompanied his boss to Snake Eyes, reached into his pocket and pulled out a folded sheet of paper. He cleared his throat. "This is our menu of services: Punching: one dollar. Both eyes blacked: three dollars. Nose and jaw broke: seven dollars. Knocked out with a blackjack: fifteen dollars. Ear chewed off: fifteen dollars. Leg or arm broke: nineteen dollars. Shot in the leg: twenty dollars. Stabbed: twenty-two dollars. Doing the big job: a hundred and up."

McTiernan added, "Be advised, if all you want are some black eyes, we're not doing much of that anymore. What will it be?"

The man leaned in and whispered, "The big job."

Shamus replied, "You have our attention. Please give all of the details to my associate. Silvy, another round."

"Yes, sir, happy to, but Blood is over in the back and wants a word with you."

"Fine. I'll be with him in a moment."

Bodee nodded to his former employer and as he took his seat in the back, two of the prostitutes from Tigress came over. "Hi, Blood, why you don't come around no more—we had some fun times, remember?"

"I do, but not tonight though. Here on business."

"Are you Juba's boy? We been taken bets on who'll break you in. Wanna go next door to Tigress? I got the best room."

"No, thank you, ma'am."

"Ooh, it's been a long time since anyone ma'am'd me. How you like to ma'am me against the wall, or how you like to ma'am me bent over a couch? You can ma'am me as much and however you want, baby, let's go!"

Blood dismissed the girls as the Whyo leader made his way to the back table.

"Shamus, sorry about overstepping the other day."

McTiernan smiled and Bodee was surprised at Blood's choice of words and tone.

"All in the heat of the moment. I did speak to my man—don't think McFarland will do anything to the boy over here."

"He found a way around your order and is coming after Bodee's girlfriend. Found out he waited outside her building and pulled her into the alley. Roughed her up some and said he'd be back."

"Blood, you and I know how to play the game, don't we? You asked me real proper—our understanding goes back years. Give me the girl's address and name."

Bodee borrowed a piece of paper from Silvy and jotted the information down and the two men left.

"What did you learn? Did you pay attention?"

"Yes, I did. You didn't threaten him—you asked him with respect, and kind of buttered him up."

"You're right. I made a mistake when you had your problem a few days ago—lost my head for a moment and went too far. He gave me a pass, but called me on it, so I had to be real calm today. I didn't cuss him out or throw any punches, but we got exactly what we wanted right away, and that is true power."

CHAPTER 29

Ready

"We made this food hours ago. Started out as a cooking lesson for Nellie. Didn't realize we'd be having company."

Juba took Nellie's hand. "We're so sorry for everything that happened, Mabel, and Nellie, pleasure to meet you. Bodee told me about you and you seem like a nice girl."

"She *is* a nice girl," Mabel corrected. Nellie took her mother's hand. "Thank you so much, Madame Juba. Please excuse my appearance—I'm not dressed proper to meet you because I'm having a terrible day."

"I understand, sweetie. We all came over to help deal with the reason for your bad day. You can drop the madame and call me Juba."

"As you please, but what's your last name?"

"My family Ashanti—no last name, but our first name has meaning."

Bodee jumped in. "Juba's first name means Monday, and"—Bodee and Juba stated in unison—"all important things happen on Monday." Everyone laughed.

Nellie turned to her boyfriend. "What your name mean? Is it Ashanti, too?"

"My name is really Bodua, and it mean protector."

Nellie snuggled close and whispered, "Are you going to be my protector?"

"What you think I'm doing here right now?"

Mabel interrupted the moment. "Enough of all this love talk. You ain't married yet. I want some space between the two of you."

"Grandma, why you never took a last name?" Bodee asked.

"Didn't want the last name of my owner. No offense to any of you, but I didn't need no more names. Not doing any kind of paperwork. Juba worked fine my whole life—don't need nothing else."

"Well, I appreciate what you sayin', but the reality is if you want to work in a job where they keep track of what they paying you, you need a surname. I was born a few years after the war ended and my mama picked ours. I understand our first president owned slaves, but my family proud to take his name because we'll give Washington some new meaning. Now, Bodee, tell me about these dreams you been having."

"That's kind of a long story."

"You done swooped into my daughter's life and changed everything. Yesterday, I didn't know you existed and today is all about Bodee Rivers. I'm not trying to be difficult, so you don't need to tell me everything. Give me the short version."

"Okay, Mrs. Washington. Sometimes I dream things and they come true. Might be something little, like I'll run into somebody somewhere or someone will choose to do one thing instead of the other. My mother told me this all non-sense, but my grandmother said people in our family did these kinds of things over the years. Anyway, I been having this vision about a ship, and I think I got a job on the same boat, and something is going to happen on the hurricane deck from what I can tell. I know this sounds crazy, but you asked."

"I sure did. Now let's finish this dinner, you two men got to go downstairs soon."

⊷⊫⊜ ⊜⊨⊷

"You want anything else to eat, Jimmy? The pie here is real tasty."

"No, I think I'm okay. Tell me about what we're doing tonight."

"We'll grab the girl out of her apartment because I doubt if she'll come down again this late at night—she lives with her ma. Don't want to kill anyone, but we need to knock the mom out. Better to do the daughter in the apartment—much more comfortable than the alley and if you want the mom, go ahead. I don't think you'll want the girl when I'm done with her, though. Understand?"

"Yeah. Whenever you're ready."

"You are the best number two."

"Yup . . . all about the double slice, and since you got the other eight slices, why don't you pay the bill?"

"Funny. I got a good feeling about this and it ain't all work, what we about to do is pure fun."

"You can say that again, Arlin!"

⊷▬◉ ◉▬◉◦

The group upstairs in the apartment finished eating, cleaned the dishes, and turned the lights out. Bodee ran through the plan in his mind as he sat on the couch—it would all be over soon. Nellie snuck out of the bedroom for a minute, sat next to Bodee, and gazed into his eyes. "Bodua, you are my protector," she said and leaned in. The moment their lips connected, a voice called out from the next room, "I told you enough of the love talk. Come back in here."

"Don't worry, Bodee going down to be with Blood. Be right in," Nellie said, and offered one last thought to the man in her life. "You better be real careful."

⊷▬◉ ◉▬◉◦

McFarland noticed the same newsie from earlier back on the block screaming, "Extra! Extra, read all about it. Marines in Tangereez," and waved him over.

"You remember me?" Arlin asked.

"No. sir. Never seen you or the woman you were with . . . I mean never saw you before in my life."

McFarland laughed. "Not the best liar, are you?"

The newsie lowered his head and his knees started to shake. McFarland continued, "Kid, I know you recognize me and I'm not going to hurt you. Here's a dollar for all your papers. I need you to leave, and don't tell nobody you saw me."

"Sure thing, mister. Don't need to ask me twice! I can do that—no problem." He threw the rest of his stack in a nearby can and ran away.

⊷▬◉ ◉▬◉◦

Blood and Bodee sat behind a crate in the alley next to Nellie's building with a full view of the two Whyos as they got up from their table, left the corner restaurant, and had a conversation with the paperboy.

"Listen up, Bodee, if everything goes like we want, things will be easy tonight—if not, we need to stop them before they enter the building. You got a bat and I got some other things. You ready?"

"Ready. No one will hurt Nellie."

"Okay, Mr. Baseball Player, they on the move. Throw the rock against the garbage can across the street." Bodee's line drive hit the can square in the center. "Damn, you can throw!"

The two Irishmen turned in the direction of the can, but didn't see anything of interest.

"Something like that might be a signal in Chicago, not like all the changing key bullshit here in New York."

"Let's first check out who threw the rock. Can't have anything happen to my new boss," Jimmy said.

McFarland liked the sound of that.

Everybody was ready as they crossed the street.

CHAPTER 30

Return to Chicago

JIMMY MCPHEE POINTED. "The rock came from the alley straight ahead—next to her building. Better check before we go up."

The two men walked over to investigate and once they were within a few steps of the gap between the buildings, McPhee shoved his new boss inside.

"What the hell! Why'd you—" McFarland stopped in midsentence as he realized all ten Whyos in his crew surrounded him.

McTiernan began the conversation. "Top of the evening to ya, Arlin. I bet you're hoping we're all here to give you a much-needed singing lesson. Have you guys ever heard anybody as tone deaf as this miserable fuck?"

All of the men laughed as they called out, "Never! He's the worst ever!"

"What is this? I did all of the dirty jobs and worked hard since I been here. Tell him, Jimmy. What's this all about?" McFarland complained.

Jimmy stepped forward. "You been here five fucking days and you had the nerve to tell me I don't have what it takes to move up? You moron, who do you think is the number two in this gang?"

"I—I don't know."

"You don't even understand the most basic shit . . . five days and you want to take over the world. I'll tell you who the number two is . . . it's me, you stupid eejit!" The men chuckled and McPhee continued, "Arlin McFarland, the man who explains how everything works, couldn't figure out the number two was assigned to him to keep an eye because of his long-standing reputation as an asshole. Be proud, everyone agrees—total asshole." Another laugh. "You can't say I didn't warn you. How do you want to do this, Shamus?"

"This is your show. Let's teach him how the sissies maintain order in the ranks."

"All right. So this is what we're going to do. Arlin over here was generous enough to promise me two slices of whatever he stole from Shamus."

McTiernan interrupted, "By the way, Jimmy told me about this right away."

McFarland finally processed his dire circumstances. "You can't do this! Do you know who my cousin is? I'm protected, you can't do this. Send me away. I'll leave and go to another city—maybe I'm not right for the Whyos . . . forget all the sissy stuff. Let me go, and you'll never see me again."

"New York was your last chance," Jimmy said. "It is a shame, though, you've got a real talent for ass kicking, but not enough to offset all the other bullshit. Back to what I was saying, you promised me two slices, so let me begin by giving them back." McPhee pulled out his switchblade and slowly slashed two long lines from the corner of McFarland's mouth to each of his ears as two other men held him.

McPhee backed away to admire his work and instructed the rest of the men to each offer their own slice wherever and however they thought appropriate. McFarland didn't even whimper.

McTiernan walked over to what was left of his new associate, bent down, and held up his head by the back of his hair. "I'll give you this much, you are one tough son of a bitch. Okay boys, let's sing one last sissy song. Don't worry, Arlin, this selection provides the best possible farewell."

The conductor raised his hand and the chants started. The men began with a whisper, and soon the full "Why-o, Why-o, Why-o" in a one-two rhythm filled the air. The leader began to provide the base in the eerie chant and all of the men converged on their victim. McTiernan lowered his right hand to end the performance, and used his left to provide the final cut.

The men dumped the body into an open box and started to leave. McTiernan called out, "Wait, boys. One last thing to do." He found a piece of wood to cover the crate and scribbled three words on the side, *Return to Chicago.*

The three women heard the knock on the door followed by, "Let us in." The men entered with smiles on their faces and Bodee pronounced, "It's over," but offered no details—not to spare the women—but because he had none to offer. He didn't know the exact fate of McFarland but accepted his uncle's explanation that the Whyos had other reasons for doing whatever they did. Mabel permitted a little love talk and Nellie hugged her protector. Juba expected to be fully briefed by her enforcer once they returned to Minetta Lane.

Bodee settled down for the night in his small cot. *I didn't do much, but I was ready—wasn't running tonight. Lived up to my name for the first time.* He fell asleep with a smile.

Part Three

June 15, 1904

CHAPTER 31

Not Afraid No More

THE WATER BECAME heavier by the minute as the relentless, pulsing waves continued to push Bodee down. Each climb back to the surface became increasingly difficult. "Over here. Over here," he cried as he extended his left arm, which caused him to sink, yet again. Finally, someone in the small boat spotted him and called out, "Hang on."

He tried to swim toward the sound of the voice and noted the image of the *Republic* in the distance. *Got to keep going. Must find the strength. People are counting on me.* A massive wave engulfed him and he tried to stay afloat, but with arms like rubber, he sank deeper. *Need to be strong. Please God, give me one more chance.* An oar pierced through the water and a man screamed, "Grab on!"

Bodee woke up on the floor of the apartment and found Juba seated across the room with a pencil and paper. "I made notes about everything you said. Tell me what happened."

"Nah, you go first," Bodee answered as he rose and walked to the water pitcher to pour himself a glass. He organized and processed his thoughts while pulling up a chair across from his grandmother. "Tell me what you wrote down."

"You kept saying, *got to find him.* You moved like you swimming and then struggling somehow, lashing out with your arms and legs. Once you settled down, you grabbed something with your right hand, lay on your back, peddled with your legs for a while, and said, *got to find him* again—you did this many times, but the struggle on the last one went on the longest. Not sure I understand this fighting part. At the end, I thought you didn't make it."

"Close to what I recall, but I don't remember having a fight with anyone."

"I been askin' you the same thing every time you wake up from these visions and you got to tell me the truth. Were you scared?"

"I never been more afraid in my life, but this is important—I pulled people to safety by fishin' them out of the water. My dreams are connected—the little boat must be a lifeboat from the *Republic* because the steamship was in the background."

"We got to think about this because now we know what will happen. I'm not sure you should go back. This sounds as bad as bad gets. Let me hold your hands. Come on over here."

Juba took his hands into hers and started her moan. "Hmmmmmmmm, hm-mmmmmmmmm." After some time, she let go, fell to the floor, and spoke in Creole. Bodee sat silently and let her finish.

Finally, her language returned to English. "Go on and get cleaned up. I'm plannin' to think on this while I make you something to eat, and we'll have a long talk before you head out to the ship—not sure you should go. Told you to call me Juba, but you got to remember you my blood, and the grandma in me says you should stay away from this ship cause it damned."

"I rescued those people. Didn't you say being a protector was my job, like my great- grandfather, Bodua?"

"Maybe so, but I don't want to lose you—this might not be the time for you to be protecting anything. How sure are you about the oar?"

"This part is clear. I almost drown, but I make it in the end."

"Oh, Bodee, what if you didn't get this part right? You understand how easy it is to read these things the wrong way. Helping Nellie last night might be enough. I missed out on twenty years of your life. Don't want to miss no more."

"We still got time—I'll try later with the trick you showed me with my third eye, or I might see more tonight."

"What if it happens today?"

"I don't know when it's going to happen, but I'm not even working on the *Republic* today."

"Let me hold your hands again."

"Nah, we done enough for now. No need. You won't miss more time with me. I promise you."

Juba studied her grandson and admired his resolve, but questioned his logic as well as his interpretation of events. The fact he wouldn't be on the troubled vessel that day was of some comfort, but the sense of mortal danger couldn't be more apparent.

"You a grown man and you got the right to do what you think best, but nothing about this feels right, and this is my gift, so I'm worried. We dodged a problem with the gangster last night, don't need something else today."

"I learned a lot about myself with the thing with Nellie, Grandma, and I was ready to act. Uncle Marcus taught me what it takes to get what you want. He said part of winning is physical, but lots of it is strategy and what's in your head. What's been in my head has been bad for a long time, but not anymore. If I'm supposed to be protecting people and if this is what my dream is all about, I'll do my part—not afraid no more."

"You still got to be careful. Last night was the first time you tested yourself, but you had Blood by your side and he been through this kind of thing many times. Even if you would have stumbled, he planned to pick you up. Who'll do this for you out in the water?"

"Not sure, but I understand what you're saying. Don't think you need to worry, though. I'll make it, but what about those other people if I'm not there to help them?"

"I get your point too, but you should think carefully about this. In the end, it's your choice. Hold onto your pepper shaker real tight today and I'll be your salt, just like I was for your mama. Go on now, but if they want you to go back to your regular ship tomorrow, promise me we'll talk first."

"Okay, I promise."

C H A P T E R 32

Hot Dog Island

"Listen, Triple N, I got to go down to the Row and get my papers. Two-Tooth Tommy can't take all these days off like you. Don't understand nothing about no paid vacation—may not be on the up and up. Probably some kind of law against it as far as I can tell, so you'll only be with Mrs. Heinricky, because I got to work. I'll see you later."

"Not Heinricky, just Heinrich, and she's softening up. I think she might give you a paid vacation, too."

"You asked her a bunch of times. Don't want you to miss out because of me."

"She needs to meet you, is all. Why didn't you come over the other day?"

"Stop asking me the same question. I told you, can't mess up my deal at work—they give me the biggest stack because I sell the best. The guy reads the headline to me before I head out and I practice a couple of times, because if you don't say it right, people won't know what you sellin' and they won't buy. The headline is the thing, so you just have to understand the one story. Remember last week when everybody screaming, 'Extra! Extra! Read all about it. Marines in Tangerie?"

"Yeah."

"Ain't no Tangeerie. I said Tangier, the right way, and I sold out."

"You think you stupid, but you the smartest person I ever met in my whole life—you understand all the important stuff. Mrs. Heinrich will like that about you. You'll see."

"She don't care about Tangier or me, but no worries."

"Once I tell her this headline thing and about how you left again last night because the lady wouldn't let me in, she'll like you and take you on the steamship. You'll love being on the water and when we go to the picnic, you can eat one of those hot dogs. Better than the pork and beans, you put mustard on top and—"

Tommy interrupted, "No hot dog for me, she don't want me. Mrs. Heinricky or whatever her name is, wants you, not me—I don't need none of that soft livin' anyways. I got my corner and my customers and I'm workin' my way up in the newspaper business. One day, I'll be the guy taking the papers off the truck and handing them out to all the newsies—I got big plans and if you still a newsie when I get the job, I'll give you everything you need."

Eddie's smile vanished. "We'll call her Mrs. H. until you learn the name right, but I think if I—"

"No more talk. I'm a newspaperman and people on the Row go to work early. Can't be late. I'll ask the man who runs the lodge to give you another chance. Later."

Tommy headed across the street and out of Eddie's view. He sat on the ground with his head between his legs and allowed the tears to flow, wiping his eyes with his sleeve. He followed Eddie at a safe distance as his friend made his way to Little Germany.

⊷▜▅◑ ◐▅▛⊶

"Come on in. We need to get you cleaned up, you're filthy—looks like you slept in the street," Gerda Heinrich said. Eddie tilted his head sideways.

She noticed the unusual reaction to her comment and realized her mistake. "Did you stay in the alley last night? You promised me you'd be inside."

"We tried, but the lady at the door thinks I'm bad and stopped me from coming in. She said I didn't have enough time to *repute* or something."

"Do you mean repent?"

"Not sure, but she hates me and grabbed me by the ear and pulled me out to the street. All the newsies laughed at me."

"Why does this woman hate you so much?"

"Says I'm the devil and she uses these long words no one understands. Calls me a *devant*."

"Do you mean deviant?"

"Yeah, I think so, don't understand what it means nohow. No one does."

"No need for you to understand these grown-up words. Why does she call you bad things?"

He lowered his head and slumped his shoulders, "Because of what happened."

"What did you do that made her angry?"

"Well, first thing, I fell asleep in school and she woke me up with a whack." He slapped his hand against the wall. "Yeah, real loud. Maybe *devant* mean I'm too tired, but this don't make sense because we all go to there to sleep."

"No, being tired wouldn't make her hate you. What else happened?"

"An older boy climbed on top of me in my bed and pulled my pants down, so I stabbed him with a ruler I made sharp. Does *devant* mean I stabbed somebody?"

She pulled him close and gave him a squeeze. "Don't you bother with what *deviant* means, you don't need to think about those things."

"Tommy helped me out and didn't go inside either. He stayed with me last night in our spot, which ain't so bad, except for the cheese smell."

"Yes, I can tell—strong cheese. You brought the foul odor with you this morning."

"Not such a bad night—we have this way we pile up the boxes. Now, I'm not sayin' we'd invite a fancy person like you over or nothing." He giggled. "Ain't so bad in the summer. Worried about the winter, though. The lady says I need to *repute* and won't let me back in 'til I do."

"Not *repute*, the word is repent, and don't worry about that word either. I don't know why you didn't come over here—you can always stay with me and perhaps by the winter we can work out something for you to stay here all the time." He offered another thousand-dollar smile and she, another hug.

"Time to wash you up and put on some new clothes. I have a few things my son wore when he was your size—should fit you. First, a bath, stinky boy!"

--->==o o==<---

Gerda started filling the bathtub and left Eddie to play while she gathered some towels. The stories about Tommy made her think, *what a nice thing for him to do, but it's one child caring for another and this isn't the way it should be, and I can't take in two of them.*

By the time she returned, his game was in full swing. "This is the steamship!" He held up the bar of soap and splashed the water. The ship rode the wave, but water spilled onto the floor. Gerda laughed as she covered the spill with towels and said, "Let's keep the waves in the tub . . . no, I mean in the river." The rocky waters settled down and he maneuvered the bar to the faucet and screamed, "Ding, ding, ding."

"What's the sound? The ship's horn?"

"Yeah, you catch on fast, but this is a bell. We stopping, for real. Do you know where, Mrs. H? Have you guessed yet?"

"Where are we?"

"Oh, no. One more wave!" Gerda's dress became soaked. "Sorry about the rough stop, but everything is okay. I finished captain school last week and I didn't fall asleep even one time. I learned all the best places to stop. Are you ready to get off?"

"Aye, aye, Captain, but where are we?" Water dripped from her hair. "Tell me soon, because I may run out of water if this goes on much longer."

"Okay, I'll slow it down. The water is choppy today, but Captain Eddie is in charge. Sorry about the waves—if that happens today, I'll put a towel over your head so your hair doesn't get wet. Don't think ladies like being in water so much, but boys love it!" He submerged his head under the water and held his breath for what seemed like an eternity. His smile bubbled up from below.

"Stop fooling around. You come up this minute, I'm . . ."

He popped up to his feet and shook his head like a wet dog.

"You're lucky I didn't put my good clothes on yet!" She splashed him back and he retrieved the soap and coasted it back to the faucet.

"Enough, we need to get ready for our day."

"All right, I'll tell all the passengers, even the ones with dripping dresses, where I put the boat."

"Silly boy, you don't *put* boats, you dock them."

"Okay, I'll tell where I docked, but first I'll ask the crew to blow the horn."

"The crew?"

"Come on, thought you was keepin' up! That's you!"

"Okay, booo booo booo."

"What kind of sound is that! You got to do better or you'll lose your job!"

"So fire me, but first say where you docked!"

"Remember, I'm in charge. Got to talk the right way to the boss."

"Sorry, Captain. Booooooo boooooo booooo."

"Better. This is the captain. I docked on . . . you sure you ready for this?"

"Yes, yes . . . tell me already!"

"I docked the ship on Hot Dog Island and we got two with mustard ready for Triple N!"

She placed one towel on his back and used another to dry his hair. "Sounds like a fun place, Eddie."

"See how I said Triple N and not Eddie. This way, everyone won't think I'm only looking out for myself!"

"So smart."

"Oh wait, one more thing to tell . . ."

"Don't ask . . . I'm ready!"

"We also got two hot dogs for Mrs. H. Eat up!"

CHAPTER 33

Father and Son

HELMUT WAGNER STOOD at his dresser and reviewed his daily to-do list—neatly printed in pencil on the back of an envelope. He walked to the mirror and checked for wrinkles in his jacket. Finally, he examined his shoes. *One more item for the list—pick up polish.* He headed down the hallway to his father's room.

Dieter Wagner stood by his window reviewing his own listing of priorities for the day.

"Father, may I borrow some black shoe polish?"

"Of course, Son." He reached into the drawer in his night table and removed a small container.

"Wait a minute, let's meet in the kitchen for coffee before you go. I want to talk."

"Yes, Father, but I did promise to arrive early to make sure we are ready for today's outing."

"I won't make you late—just give me a few more minutes." He winked. "I already polished *mine*. Start the coffee and I'll be down soon."

Helmut thought to himself. *He wants to ask me the same "what kind of" questions over and over. What kind of life will this give you? What kind of income will you earn? Always asks the same things, but never hears my answers. I don't have time for this today.*

"Of course, Father," he replied as he returned to his thoughts of all of the remaining arrangements for the event. The biggest concern—the band, the same one who stood him up on Saturday. *They better show up today.* A ride on a steamship and an all-day picnic without music would ensure a bad experience for all. *The musicians better show.*

Dieter walked to the stove to pick up the coffeepot and poured two cups, heaping two tremendous spoons of sugar and almost a third of a glass of milk into each. Both men sat at the table and leaned in to blow on their hot beverages. Each lowered their heads at the same moment before their first sip and then glanced up and chuckled. Other than their constant disagreement about the course of Helmut's career, father and son were the same in all respects—appearance, mannerisms, likes and dislikes. Most importantly, they each considered the other to be their best friend.

Both men took a mouthful of coffee and moaned "ahhh" as if cued by a conductor. They laughed again, but the father's brow crinkled, which made the son sit up straight in his chair.

"Son, we need to talk about your future."

Helmut rolled his eyes. "Oh, Father, we've done this so many times. Your thoughts on this topic are not a mystery. Why can't you understand this is the life I want? Why can't you support me?"

"The shop was profitable enough to provide for the three of us . . ." Dieter took a moment as he remembered his lovely wife, Emily, who passed away on Helmut's tenth birthday. After clearing his throat, he continued, "Yes, it took care of us for many years. Soon, I want to retire and pass the business to you."

"Father, if this were my dream as well, I would be more than happy to take over for you, but there are so many other people in the family who are interested. Three of my cousins work with you—Gustav, in particular, would love to buy the shop and take over."

"Yes, but I always hoped you would come to your senses and decide to take advantage of this opportunity."

"The business did provide for all of us, but this is not what I want to do with my life. You've always given me approval for all of the significant things I've done—the one exception should not be something of such importance."

"This is why I wanted to talk to you today. I understand you will not follow in my footsteps, so I'm selling the business to Gustav and he will pay me off monthly over the next ten years. This money, along with my savings, should be enough for me to live."

"Excellent news, Father. I'm so happy you will be able to enjoy yourself while you are still in good health. So are you saying you will be proud to have a reverend as a son?"

"Yes, I will be as proud as a father can be. I give you my blessing and when you finish your education and begin to work, I will move to the location of your assignment. I'm hoping you'll be a family man soon with a little room in your house for the grandfather of your children."

"Oh, you are moving fast . . . married with children?" Helmut laughed and pulled the envelope from his pocket. "Let me check, no, not at the top, not in the middle or at the end . . . sorry, Father, a wife and kids didn't make my list today!"

"Hopefully, it will before I'm too old. Our family is small—we need to make it bigger and stay together."

"Thank you, Father, this means so much to me. Does this also mean you'll change your instructions to Reverend Haas, so he'll stop giving me such a hard time?"

"You caught me!"

"Yes, I did."

"I hope everything goes well today. Sorry I can't go, but it's a weekday . . . much to do."

"I understand, Father. I'll come by later today to congratulate my cousin on his new business venture. Perhaps we can all go out to dinner."

"An outstanding idea. Now, where's my polish?"

"I'll replace the one I borrowed with a new one later today, Father." The son waved his envelope at his father, who waved his own in return. Another laugh. Both finished their last drop of coffee, offered one last sigh in unison, and left the apartment with a sense of relief and resolution. They headed their separate ways for the day after agreeing to part professionally, but both had a feeling their new understanding would prove to be the thing that would keep them together, instead of being the only thing that ever kept them apart.

Chapter 34

The East Side Docks

Bodee made a full circle, but still had plenty of time before the start of his workday. The street sign read East Third Street. *Where is the entrance?* He pulled from his pants the paper Duane had given him and his pepper shaker fell to the ground. The address on the paper agreed with his instructions. He picked up and rubbed his shaker. *What should I do, Juba?*

The streets bustled at this early hour of the morning and he spotted dozens of families walking in their Sunday finest—full suits for the men and high-collared dresses for the women.

Once a wagon pulled away from the adjacent corner, a handwritten poster attached to a street sign became visible—*17th Annual St. Mark's Picnic.* One of the well-dressed women motioned as she said, "This way." Bodee clutched his pepper shaker one last time and returned it to his pocket. *Thanks, Juba.* Another sign on the next block confirmed the correct path, and then he came upon a young man standing on the corner affixing yet another marker. *Helmut?* He was tempted to run toward his new acquaintance, but didn't because the man was White. *Better go slow, don't want no trouble.*

He called out, "Helmut?" The man tapped a small nail to post his sign and turned. "Bodee Rivers, my savior! I hoped you'd be assigned to us today. The steamship is around this bend."

"Been walking around in circles for a while."

"Not so tricky, the East Third Street Pier is on . . . guess what? East Third!" Helmut chuckled. "I'm only putting these signs up to make people feel welcome. Did you have any more problems with my friend after I introduced the two of you?"

"No, he hired me right away. Still waiting to do my payroll papers, though, but I already worked a few days. This job will give me what I need for the summer. Can't thank you enough—this really helped me out." He grabbed his pepper shaker firmly in his right hand as he pulled out his otherwise empty pockets for effect. His one quarter, all that remained of the money his mama left him, fell to the ground.

Helmut pointed. "Better pick that up right away—looks like your entire fortune is about to roll into the gutter!"

Bodee laughed as he chased after his runaway coin. "Appreciate you looking out."

"Well, you took care of me on Minetta Lane. This is the least I could do. I'm worried about you not doing the paperwork yet. My friend tends to like a little free labor up front."

"Yeah, one of the other workers told me the same thing happened to him. I'll ask the first mate about the stuff I need to fill out."

"Wise move, my friend. Don't let him get away with anything."

Bodee smiled. *This is the first White man who ever called me a friend.* "No problem if I miss out on a little pay, but I need to give this quarter some company real soon, if you understand my meaning!" The two men laughed and he continued, "The job is the best—I like the other porter and he's showing me the ropes with painting and cleaning, mostly outdoors. Can't you see my sunburn?"

Helmut glanced down and paused for a second. "Funny. How is everything else going?"

Bodee wanted to tell his new friend about Nellie and the dream along with his sense of danger, but decided to remain silent—most of what he would explain was unbelievable and a Black man had to be careful not to overstep with a White man. "Everything is fine. How about you?" he said.

Helmut wanted to provide the good news about his father giving him permission to enter the seminary, but he had just met Bodee, and no matter how close he felt, his new friend wasn't even aware of his ongoing issue with his dad—mentioning anything might be strange at this point. He answered, "Everything is fine with me, too."

A sign he had posted at the previous intersection blew away from the pole. "Oops, I think one of my signs is trying to chase your coin," Helmut said. "Got to go fix it. See you later."

Bodee watched him walk away and wondered if they'd find time to talk later. He remembered Saturday in Tompkins Square Park and smiled. *Time for work.*

He headed for the last turn and noted a group congregating below a sign— *East Third Street Recreation Pier.* The crowd's formal attire matched those he observed in the park on Saturday. *Got to be hot as hell.*

Bodee made his way through the crowd and yelled, "I'm a porter on board. Need to report for work." When the people cleared and the security officer opened the gate, the steamship came into view. *Can't be. Not today. Duane told me I'd be on the sister ship.* His mind began racing and his sense of fear bubbled to the top—it was the *Grand Republic.*

"Listen, boy. You said you needed to go to work. I can't keep this open if you not passing through," the guard said.

Bodee turned and stammered, "This is the *Grand Republic* from the West Side. I'm supposed to be on another Knickerbocker boat."

"Boy, this is the *General Slocum* and it docks here lots of times over the summer. Are you coming through or not?"

"You're wrong."

"Who the hell are you to tell me I'm wrong? I work here every damn day and I'm not holding this open any longer for some lost Darkey. This is owned by Knickerbocker, but it is the *General Slocum.* This is your last chance. You coming through or not?"

Every bone in Bodee's body told him to turn around and head back to the Bend. *Not ready for this today, thought I had more time.* Bodee reluctantly walked past the officer.

Once he approached the gangway, he detected a different color of paint on the hull as compared to the *Republic,* as well as a different type of railing. The sign read, *The General Slocum Welcomes St. Mark's*—the guard was right, but Bodee's sense of dread increased with every step he took in the direction of the massive vessel.

CHAPTER 35

The General Slocum

BODEE ARRIVED A few minutes late, but still decided to tour the main level before reporting to the lamp room. *This is just like the Republic, same exact layout but everything is in slightly better condition.* Knickerbocker had two boats with the same design. Stenciled lettering on the faded canvas coverings on the life preservers read, "Passed Inspection June 18, 1891," which made him question his initial impression of *newness.* After scratching a discolored spot on the wall with his fingernails, he noted many layers of both paint and varnish—exactly what he'd come to expect on the *Republic.* The voice came from behind. "Excuse me, young man, who are you and what are you doing?"

Bodee turned and found a man in full uniform with an air of authority. He stood at attention before offering his response. "Sir, my name is Bodee Rivers. I'm a porter on loan from the *Grand Republic* for today's excursion. Found something here I thought I should touch up."

"Okay, Mr. Rivers. I like your initiative. Already looking for things to do. This is what we need—she's a grand old boat, but does need a little attention every once in a while. I'd imagine, though, she's in better shape than what you're used to. The *General Slocum* was commissioned in 1891, and your ship about twelve years prior. What do you think of my baby?"

"She's beautiful, sir. Shines in the morning sun."

"She sure does. I'm Captain Van Schaik, but let me connect you with your real boss, our first mate." He formed a cone with his hands and called out to a man in the distance, "Flanagan, over here."

Edward Flanagan hurried over. "Sir, is this man causing a problem?"

"No. No. This is a new crew member who needs to be settled in, but please provide him with our standard welcome remarks."

The first mate took a deep breath and turned toward his new report, nostrils flaring. "Yes, sir. You're going to be with us for the day. Be advised there'll be no slacking on board. The *Slocum* is the jewel of the Knickerbocker fleet." He turned to the captain. "Sorry, sir, I meant to say the jewel of all of New York."

Van Schaik smiled. "Keep going."

"She's named after the famous Civil War hero and was . . . sorry, Captain . . . is . . . the best in her class in New York." He paused, hoping he'd said enough.

"And . . ." Van Schaik said.

"And . . . the man standing before you has been at the helm from the beginning."

"This means I'm plenty old, young man, but also experienced—not a situation or a place on these waters I haven't encountered and dealt with. Do your job well, and we might put in a good word with your Captain Pease and perhaps one day you'll be permanent crew on Knickerbocker's finest." He winked as he walked away and the first mate offered an obligatory chuckle.

"What the hell are you doing up here? Stay the fuck away from the captain—the only thing you need to know is what to do next. You already made me say all this shit that don't matter nohow. You supposed to be down below ten minutes ago. Don't let me find you causing any more trouble today."

"Sorry, sir."

"Don't sir me. You call me Flanagan. No, don't call me anything at all—just do your fucking job! Now go on."

Bodee proceeded downstairs while his supervisor rushed off mumbling under his breath, "Always makes me say this speech like I'm some trained monkey. I'm tired of this—he says he's too old—well, this is getting real old for me."

⊶═◉ ◉═⊷

Bodee found the head porter standing with another man outside the lamp room with his shoulder against the door. "Hi, Duane sent me for the day."

"Your day started fifteen minutes ago, Bodee. I'm Walter Payne and this is the oiler, Elbert Gaffga—he's helping me get this door open because you nowhere to be found, but now you can do the pushin' with me. We still got no light, Elbert. Can you hold your lamp up so we can see?"

"Sure thing, but you got to hurry up. I got my own work."

"Let's do this, Bodee. Something blocking the door on the other side."

The men pushed against the door, which barely opened. At the peak of their effort, the obstruction became dislodged and both men fell through the doorway, knocking over an open bucket of varnish, which splattered on the floor. Bodee searched for something to pick up the spillage. The room came into view as Gaffga moved around the small windowless space. Clothing hung from the walls on pegs and scraps of wood sat beneath a shelf loaded with oil-based paint. Cans of kerosene for the boat's lanterns occupied one corner and jars of polish for the brass fixtures sat in another. The floor was scattered with debris. Bodee picked up a piece of cloth and dipped it into the spill.

"What you doing?"

"Got to take care of this—the varnish spilled all over the floor."

"Look around . . . do you think we spend lots of time cleaning up down here? Didn't Duane teach you nothing?"

Bodee gazed again at the room, which appeared to be a dumping ground for various supplies. Walter stated the obvious. "We worry about the rest of the boat. More than enough to do up top. No one gonna ever see this mess but you and I. Not even Flanagan comes down here. This ain't the first spill down here and it ain't gonna be the last."

"Okay."

"Someone came down here last night—the place looks shittier than normal. Yesterday, I stacked cases of glasses down here for the German trip today. See the hay all over the floor?"

"Yeah."

"Well that's from the packing materials for the glassware. Someone must've been in here this morning."

"Listen, I got to go. You better light a lantern. I'm leaving," Elbert said.

"Thanks, I'll talk to you later. Take this container and start filling the lamps."

The oiler left and Bodee complained, "Wait, can't hardly see in here."

Walter struck a match to light another lantern, blew it out, and tossed it against the wall. "Over there," he pointed. "And you better not claim it's too heavy for you. You one skinny boy."

"Don't need no help." Bodee bent his legs before lifting the drum and headed up the stairs as Wayne lit another lantern, stepping on the match with the heel of his shoe. Walter stuck his head out of the door and grinned as his helper for the day struggled with the first set of steps, "And Duane told me about your daydreaming—better not let any of the bosses catch you."

Bodee took each step slowly and kept his head down as he did his best to avoid falling. Spilling oil on the stairs would be a major mistake and require a time-consuming cleanup. Bodee wanted to start with the lamps on the lower decks in order to lighten his load as he climbed, but after the rude greeting he received from his coworker, he was not about to deviate from his instructions. Once on the hurricane deck, he carefully placed the drum on the floor, and raised his head for the first time.

"My God!" he exclaimed as he sprung up and ran to the interior. He tried to take it all in—the black chairs and tables with only the center tabletop covered in gold. *This hurricane deck has the exact layout from my vision. I thought the different furniture was a meaningless detail, but I should have known.* A feeling of trepidation came over him and he called out, "How could I have misread this?" He rushed to the open service door, and pulled it back halfway and read, "*SS Slocum.*" The *SS*, just like his dream, but his assumption of what followed those letters couldn't have been more wrong. Bodee realized today was the day and the *Slocum*, not the *Republic*, was the ship. Whatever extra time he had to prepare vanished, and whatever was about to happen would take place over the next few hours.

CHAPTER 36

Boarding

"OVER HERE, GERDA. Thank God you're here to help. So many people arrived early and they won't let us board until after eight. People were wandering all over the streets, so I put up signs directing them here. Welcome!"

"Sorry, Helmut. I would have been here earlier, but I needed to prepare my guest for the day. Do you remember Eddie from the park on Saturday?"

"Of course, the hot dog lover!" Eddie's small grin blossomed into a full-fledged smile as he asked the obvious follow-up question. "You got any ready right now?"

"You ate your breakfast in the apartment this morning and people don't barbecue at seven thirty in the morning, but they'll be served later."

"Promise?"

"Yes, and I'll also let you try some strudel, which I think is tastier than a hot dog!"

"This I gotta see, nothin's better than a hot dog!"

Gerda turned to Helmut. "Don't you worry, we'll hand out the programs and, yes, I do have all of the information about the events and if they ask about the boat, the little note you gave me is right here." She pulled a scrap of paper out of her pocketbook. "The *General Slocum* is a dual-side-wheel, three-deck steamer with a maximum capacity of twenty-five hundred people. The vessel is thirteen years old and is one of the finest steamships in New York. How did I do?"

"Not bad at all. Another group is headed our way, please speak with them, and by the way, the pamphlets are terrific, but why didn't you shorten the ti-tle—the *Journal for the Seventeenth Annual Excursion of St. Mark's Evangelical Lutheran Church* is a bit long." They both laughed. The document, written in English and

German, contained over a hundred ads, menus, and a few jokes. Helmut corrected himself. "Actually, the long name works. Excellent job."

Helmut turned as he heard footsteps from behind.

"Good morning to my two organizers."

"Good morning, Reverend Haas."

"Allow me to introduce my old friend from the seminary. Reverend George Schultze from Erie, Pennsylvania. Back at school, he was *George the Giant*." Reverend Haas laughed as he remembered his days as a student.

Helmut extended his hand. "A pleasure to meet you. My name is Helmut Wagner and this is Gerda Heinrich. Welcome to the 17th Annual Excursion of St. Mark's. Did I say it right, Gerda?"

"Almost."

Reverend Schultze chuckled. "The name is a mouthful, perhaps befitting such a grand event." He shook Helmut's hand and tipped his hat to Gerda. "And who might this young man be who is hiding behind your dress?" Eddie leaned to the side so only his head was visible and he stuck his tongue out at the visiting minister, who smiled and managed to snatch Eddie up into the air with one careful swing of his right arm. Schultze threw his new friend well over his head. "So you think you can stick your tongue out to a man from Pennsylvania, do you? Well, I'll show you what we do to little boys like you." The jovial giant tossed him again and cradled Eddie to his chest. "You're one funny little boy. What's your name?"

"Eddie, but they call me Triple N at work."

"Work? With a nice mommy like yours, I'm surprised you need a job." No one felt the need to offer a correction. He continued, "Well, Triple N, it was fun throwing you about." The minister winked. "And you better stay alert when we get to Long Island, because I might sneak up behind you and . . ."

Gerda pulled Eddie close and everyone laughed.

⊷➡◼ ◼⬅⊶

Tommy found a convenient spot across the street from the pier and sat on a wooden crate, playing a game in the spirit of the day, which involved tossing a baseball against the brick wall of the adjacent building. The sound of the ball against the wall thrilled him and he imagined the sound of a baseball being hit by a proper bat. A man opened a second-story window and called out, "Stop all the noise—don't need this shit."

Tommy repositioned his seat and peered across the way at his friend. He shrieked, "One . . . two . . . three," and thought, *The big guy flung Triple N three times!* The man in the window responded, "And shut the fuck up—working people are sleeping up here!"

The crate, now at the edge of the building, provided a superb view of his guttersnipe walking away hand-in-hand with Mrs. Heinrich. Tommy understood the look—the same one he'd seen on the faces of the other mothers as they congregated on the dock. *Triple N will be fine. Time for work.* One more toss of the ball directly into the window of the man who complained. Two-Tooth walked out of the alley with his head down. The man rushed back to the window, "Goddam pain in the ass. Better not come back here . . ." Tommy didn't hear a word he said.

⋆─▣ ▣─⋆

At 8:15 a.m., Van Schaik gave first mate, Edward Flanagan, the signal, and he blew the big horn. The schedule listed cast-off at 8:45 a.m. Flanagan turned and called to one of his men, "Coakley, come over here and give a tour to our friends from the police before we begin greeting the passengers." People formed a line.

"Right away, sir. Follow me, officers."

Knickerbocker hired two policemen, Albert Van Tessel and Charles Kelk, for the day as additional security. The men expected a day in the sun in which their most difficult task might be to control an inebriated husband. They whispered, "Only a few men today . . . this will be easy." The trio headed down the staircase.

"I'm showing you this part so you'll understand the steamship, but only employees go down below. This is the lamp room, where we keep supplies, and the engine room is back this way with two boilers with lots of coal. Any questions?"

"This sure is some piece of machinery," Van Tessel said.

"Yeah, she's getting old, but her heart is brand new—a WA Fletcher, the best in the business. The *Slocum* used to be the best too, but this old lady is well past her prime. We do try to keep up appearances. Let's go up top."

After the three men toured the first two decks, they climbed the last set of stairs to the hurricane deck. Officer Kelk walked toward the harbor side. "The railing appears to be less than three feet."

"No sir, it is a full three feet, but don't worry—city folk are careful. Believe me, they stay far away from the edge. I don't think more than a handful of the people on this boat can swim. No one is looking to go overboard."

"Yes, I see how they're all dressed—I don't think this group is planning on splashing around the water too much today," Van Tessel said.

The crew blew the horn again and the two reverends boarded next, taking positions on either side of the captain so they could extend greetings.

"Strong turnout, Reverend Haas," Van Schaik remarked.

"Yes, we expect a total of almost fifteen hundred. Here they come."

John Coakley returned to the first mate, who handed him a mechanical clicker and said, "Remember, click once for each adult and once for every two children under the age of fourteen—can't go over twenty-five hundred."

"Yes, sir."

The St. Mark's parishioners entered the gangway in a most orderly and respectable fashion. Coakley began clicking and the captain's mind wandered as he studied the crowd. *Isn't this a trip to a picnic? They're dressed more for a wedding or a funeral. So odd.* The majority of the men didn't attend because of a conflict with typical Wednesday work hours, but the few present wore full suits and ties. The women sported long dresses, which afforded full coverage along with fancy hats. The children donned similar clothing, but most of the boys cuffed their pants while some girls hitched up their skirts for more freedom of movement. Smiles were the order of the day and the items carried onboard documented expectations—baseball gloves, balls, bats, toys, and dolls. Some of the young boys clutched empty glass jars—their goal to catch a frog or a firefly as a trophy to bring back to the city. The day was going to be memorable, indeed.

CHAPTER 37

Am I German Yet?

"Reverend Haas, may I speak with you when you're finished offering greetings? I only need a minute."

"Sure, Helmut, but many people are running late—I'm still waiting for my family. Everyone is coming except for my son, George, who will be missed, but everyone else will be here—my sister, sister-in-law, and nephew, along with my wife, Anna, and my sweet Gertrude. Have you seen any of them?"

"Yes, sir, everyone except for your wife and daughter."

"All right, I asked the captain to allow more time for people to board, so I do have a few minutes, but please don't tell me how this is going to be the best day ever or something else along those lines."

"No, sir, I understand you don't want any more grand statements. I've got excellent news about my father and me—we spoke this morning about my future."

"I understand your father wants you to take over the butcher shop. Remember, fathers naturally want their children to receive what they've worked so hard to build. Why isn't this an option for you? You can still be active at St. Mark's."

"Yes, but Father gave me his blessing to enroll in the seminary. So long as you give me a strong recommendation, I think I can pursue my dream of being a Lutheran minister."

"Sometimes we hear what we want to hear, and I hope your dad did say and mean those words, but it is hard to imagine things would change so quickly. The other day he asked me . . ." Haas paused.

"To give me a hard time and discourage me from going into the church. You took this job seriously." Helmut smiled.

"It killed me, but your father and I go back years, and I tried to help the two of you come to some resolution. So let's at least say your father shifted his stance on this issue, and if he moved all the way to agreeing with your plan, I will give you the best recommendation ever!"

"Careful . . . the best ever? You don't want to overpromise."

Haas smirked. "Let's go speak to our guests."

Juba sat at the back table in the parlor and didn't realize Marcus had followed her downstairs. She moaned and first summoned the spirits. She sang the song of Marassa.

> "Marassa nou nan nwa e (bis)
> Marassa Ginen nou nan nwa devan bondye
> Dossou Marassa pote chandel pou klere nou."

Marcus took a seat and reached for her left hand, which was closest to him, but she offered her right hand instead and they exchanged an awkward embrace.

"What's wrong?"

"It's happening now."

Marcus didn't understand and again went for her left hand. She waved him off, but opened her left to reveal the saltshaker. "Can't be by your side, Bodua. You will be tested. Wish I had more time to prepare you, but no worries, you like my daddy, and I'm gonna be praying for you." She closed the shaker into the palm of her left hand and held it to her breast. "I'll be your salt, baby, don't you worry."

Professor George Maurer stood alone on the main afterdeck as he waited for the rest of the musicians to arrive. The band was hired to play music both on the boat as well as at the picnic grounds. Most members of the community worshipped at

St. Mark's, so the annual excursion afforded an opportunity to be with his family and friends while still earning a day's pay. His wife, Margaret, and his two daughters, twelve-year-old Clara and fourteen-year-old Matilda, stood by his side. The passengers surrounding him seemed ready for entertainment, so the professor clapped his hands and began to yodel.

"Oh-di-lay-ee-oh. Oh-di-lay-ee-oh
Oh-di-lay-ee-oh. Oh-di-lay-ee-oh
Oh-di-lay-ee-oh. Oh-di-lay-ee-oh."

The St. Mark's group loved to yodel and the open space in front of Maurer became a dance floor. Several of the young boys formed a circle and danced the schuhplattler. The tallest boy entered the center and rotated his body while slapping his thighs. Next, he dropped to the ground on his knees, then jumped up while hurling his hat in the air. The audience gave him a rousing round of applause, but none of the other boys immediately took their turn. Eddie took advantage of the moment and grabbed the boy's hat as he leaped into the middle of the circle. His first body rotation made him stumble and the spectators roared—he got up with a smile and slapped his thighs and knees while rubbing the area of impact from his fall. The comedy routine ended with him falling back while throwing his hat and screaming, "Oh-di-lay-ee-oh."

Two boys picked Eddie up on their shoulders as the dancing resumed. He called out to Gerda Heinrich, "Am I German yet, Mrs. H?" The boys answered for her, "Ja!"

Gerda provided confirmation, "Ja, Eddie. Yes, you are—this is for sure." The musicians settled into their spots, Maurer raised his baton, and the music followed—Gerda Heinrich felt alive for the first time in a long while.

⊷═◉ ◉═↢

The realization hit Bodee hard—he had misinterpreted his vision. The only sure way to survive was to do what he'd always done—run away as fast as possible. He left the steamship undetected and sat across from the dock staring at the countless women and children boarding for what promised to be a fun day. *I'm one man, how can I stop this? No one will listen to me. All I can do is protect myself. Will the* Slocum *crash into something or will a fire cause the disaster? I don't know and I won't be able to explain what I mean.* He gazed up at the sky. *Please help them through this—I'm safe, but safe is weak.* Bodee looked down and then popped up with his head raised toward the sky. He asked, "Why can't I live up to my name? Why do I always run away when things get tough? Why am I such a goddamn coward?"

⤙▬ ▬⤚

The match Walter Payne tossed on the bench of the lamp room at 6:45 a.m. rolled onto the floorboards and moved about as the vessel gently rocked back and forth. The varnish on the floor also tried to find its final resting place as it spread in the vicinity of the bench. The match artfully dodged contact with the spill but connected intermittently with a small splinter of wood. This periodic connection served to keep the ember alive. At 9:00 a.m., the wake from a passing ship caused both the match and the wood to roll into the spill and the otherwise soon-to-die ember found a second life. Now at 9:20 a.m., lack of fresh air in the windowless room would extinguish the spark again.

⤙▬ ▬⤚

Bodee stopped in his tracks right after beginning his walk home, turned, and glanced back. The festive music made him lower his head—he couldn't look at the celebrating parishioners who didn't understand the terrible fate about to befall them. *My God, what about Helmut?* Images of Nellie and Juba appeared in his third eye and he remembered Uncle Marcus's basic question: *Are you giving up or fighting?* Bodee asked himself, *How will I ever be any help to anyone like this?* He walked up to the security booth and surprised the officer, who pointed to a lantern which had splattered on the ground, and asked, "Did they send you for the cleanup? Been waiting a long time." No response from Bodee. "What's wrong with you, boy? Are you here for this? Did you bring something to pick up the pieces?"

"No."

The man went to a nearby storage shed and came out with a bucket and a broom. You can use these." The horn blew, announcing the imminent departure. "Hurry up or you won't be able to reboard in time."

Bodee realized this was his way back onboard. "Okay, I'll bring your stuff back when I'm done."

He swept up the debris, kept the frame of the lantern, and returned the bucket. "Thanks, mister, here's what I borrowed. Got to go."

"You better walk fast. They supposed to be shipping out in a few minutes."

Bodee headed up the ramp and found Ed Flanagan waiting for him as he reboarded the *General Slocum*.

"What the hell are you doing out here?"

"I cleaned up the mess from the lamp." He held up the frame as proof.

"How did you know? I forgot to pass along the word."

"One of the crew sent me. Not sure of all the names yet."

Flanagan nodded. "All right, back to work. We're about to head out. What's your name again?"

"Bodua."

CHAPTER 38

Casting Off

NEED TO THINK. Should I tell the first mate or the captain what's going to happen? Chances are they'll think I'm crazy. I can't let them force me to leave the ship, because I'll save at least a few people and I owe it to them to stay on board. Not sure what to do—if they'd listen to me, everyone will be saved, but why would they believe me?

Walter Payne interrupted Bodee's thoughts. "Where the hell you been? I ain't seen you for hours. Searched all over, ain't no time for this nonsense. Where you been? Answer me."

"Sorry, first I filled up the lamps up top and then they asked me to go dockside to clean up some broken glass from a lantern." Bodee held up the frame as proof.

"Who are *they*? Who asked you to go to the dock?"

"I don't know everybody's name."

"What do you mean you don't know their name?"

"This is my first day and I'm not only a porter, I'm the new porter—anybody on the crew can tell me what to do, but I didn't ask the name of the one who did."

"You flat out lying—I took care of the upper level and found the oil, but not you. Tell me the truth. I think you did leave because I looked all over for you, but I don't think anybody asked you. I'll ask you one more time, where you been?"

"Okay, I had this real bad vision—"

Walter jumped in. "Ain't got time for daydreams! Duane told me about this shit and I warned you. This is the last time we talk about dreams or this will be the last time you ever work for Knickerbocker. Which way you want this to go? Once Flanagan speaks to Gilbride, you'll lose your job on the *Republic*. Now, you go to the restaurant while I go back to the lamp room, and count on me coming up in a few minutes to check on you."

So much for the idea of telling him. Bodee hoped he would run into Helmut along the way. *Yes, he'll understand, and they'll pay attention to him because he's a White man.*

⚬⟞▤◉ ◉▤⟝⚬

"Captain Van Schaik, thank you for showing my colleague and me the pilot house. The *General Slocum* is very impressive, indeed."

"To be honest, she was the best in New York back in 1891. Today, she's showing her age, but she has lots of character. I've been at the helm from the beginning and I know every inch of her."

"A crew member told me you just received a prestigious award," Reverend Schultze said. "What was it for?"

The captain pointed to a plaque on the wall. "I've been on these waters for fifty years. Been on more boats than just the *Slocum*. Seen a lot and done a lot."

Haas walked over and read the inscription. "This award is presented to Captain William Van Schaik in recognition of transporting thirty million passengers without a fatality. Masters, Mates, and Pilots Association, 1903."

"Yes, I'm proud of the fact that after all of these years, there isn't much I haven't seen. In my opinion, it isn't so much the equipment that matters in an emergency, it's the knowledge and experience of the people in charge that makes the difference."

"Ah, yes, excellent point," Haas said as he noticed his wife and daughter among the final people to board. "My family has arrived, George, and I'm going to need some time alone with them, but don't worry—I'll let you meet them in a little while." He turned to Van Schaik. "I'll introduce you as well. Please stop by and say hello when you can."

"Will do, later for sure."

⚬⟞▤◉ ◉▤⟝⚬

George Maurer and his group prepared to perform the popular song "Unser Kaiser Friedrich" at the moment the horn reminded everyone that departure time was near. The musicians positioned themselves on the afterdeck portion of the promenade deck and the professor had a moment before they performed—enough time for a word with his family. "Sweetie, stay up here with us and keep an eye on Matilda. She seems to be interested in the Steinway boy, and I'm not so sure about him. Stay by the bandstand—the view is best from up here anyway—take the spot over there, but be alert. I can't lead the men and block you from falling into the river at the same time!" he kidded.

His wife of many years hugged her protective husband and gave him a peck on the cheek. "Always so thoughtful, dear, and yes, I'll keep an eye on Matilda. Get yourself ready; all of these people want to hear the famous George Maurer Band playing their favorites."

The children crowded around the railing as the steamship departed. Some parents urged the boys and girls to keep their distance from the edge, but others joined the fray and tried to find a free place to wave goodbye to those on the shore. Gerda Heinrich offered words of caution. "Children! Remember, we Germans do so many things well, but swimming isn't one of them! Be careful or you'll wind up overboard!" The boys ignored her advice and she joked, "Eddie, you too. From what I understand the Irish don't swim much better than the Germans!" Reverend Schultze made his way to the main deck and noted Eddie's disappointment. "All right, my young friend. Hop on here." He extended his arm and hoisted Eddie onto his broad shoulders for the best view of anyone. Triple N screamed, "I'm on top of the world."

→═◦ ◦═←

"Anna, I worried about you. How would it look if the reverend's wife and daughter didn't show up for the most significant church event of the year?"

Thirteen-year-old Gertrude Haas tilted her head and smiled at her father. "Don't be upset with us, Father. We stopped to try on the dress you said I could buy. Remember, you said once Sunday school ended for the year, I could purchase a dress as a beginning-of-summer present."

"Beginning-of-summer present—interesting. I guess we'll see."

Gertrude smiled again and her father winked. Anna offered a smile of her own and added, "Yes, George, don't be mad. I told you about the errands we needed to run this morning. Although, I may not have mentioned they involved clothing for Gertrude."

"Yes, you did seem to leave that part out!"

"Many apologies, but I thought for sure you would hold the boat a few extra minutes for the two ladies in your life."

"Yes, you're right about that. Let's all head up the stairs—the best place to see the city from the ship. We'll be casting off soon. See?" The Haas family realized the gangway was already up and the *Slocumumum* pulled out on the river. "Let's go."

Payne approached the lamp room door, but heard his name being called from above. "Walter, we've got some bad spills in the serving area. We need you right away."

He turned to go upstairs, but then opened the door about a quarter-way. "One minute, sir."

Flanagan commanded, "I said now, and I'm not going to ask you again."

The frustrated porter closed the door and grumbled as he climbed the stairs, "Nothing's going right today—this new guy threw everything off—he's no help at all. Can't do a damn thing."

"Helmut, I need to tell you something—should have told you before."

"Me too, Bodee, I wanted to tell you something important about my conversation with my father when we spoke early this morning. He agreed I can go to the seminary! All of my plans are coming together! This is going to be the best day ever." A young boy ran up and asked, "Mr. Wagner, you seen my mother? She told me to wait for her by the gangway, and I did, but never saw her."

"Yes, Peter, I did. I saw her on the highest level. She is on board."

"Thanks. Are you going to play some ball today? Should be fun."

Helmut nodded to the boy and turned to Bodee. "Sorry, so many questions and situations—what did you want to tell me?"

"What I need to tell you is bad. I—"

The voice came from behind. "Bodee Rivers. You ain't supposed to be talking to the guests, you should be cleaning. Start with the mess on the floor. You ain't done hardly anything since you boarded this morning," Payne barked.

Helmut winked at his friend, nodded, and turned to Walter. "So sorry, this is all my fault. I asked him for directions."

"Okay, but now he needs to work."

⊷▰◌ ◌▰⊶

The horn sounded and Flanagan asked Coakley for the official count.

"Nine hundred and eighty-two boarded, sir."

"Probably means close to fourteen hundred, given the number of kids. Go back inside for your regular duties."

Coakley was pleased with the nonspecific instruction and decided to take a break. He headed to the bar for the first of many complimentary mugs of beer he intended to enjoy throughout the day.

The parishioners crammed together on the pier side on each deck to bid farewell to the city for the day. The prospect of baseball, kite flying, and plenty of delicious German food and beer had everyone in the best of moods. The music provided the energy for the festive atmosphere that permeated the *General Slocum*. The ember in the lamp room began a celebration of its own as the burst of air from Walter Payne's partial opening of the door gave it another lease on life. The slow but steadily burning ember became a flame. But it required another spurt of air to realize its great potential.

CHAPTER 39

The Ship's Afire

"SHE'S AWAY, SIR," the pilot reported to the captain.

"All right, let's bring her downriver to the Williamsburg Bridge and then swing her around and proceed upriver to the Long Island Sound."

"Yes, sir."

The throngs of merry churchgoers waved to onlookers on the shore as they enjoyed being the center of attention. A bell clanged in the engine room as the *Slocum* prepared to make a one-hundred-eighty-degree turn once at the bridge. The chief engineer charged his staff to generate more steam, and the steamship surged ahead.

The sudden increase in speed made Eddie lurch forward and laugh. "Thanks for bringing me, Mrs. H. I ain't ever had this much fun."

She patted his head. "Hold on, Eddie."

John Coakley gripped his first beer of the day and stood by the stairway leading down below, trying to stay out of sight. A young boy pointed down and said, "Smoke is coming up from down there." The crewman rested his glass on the floor and walked down the staircase expecting to find steam, but he detected the distinctive odor of smoke and followed the scent straight to the lamp room. Coakley touched the knob lightly to make sure it wasn't hot, and opened the door to investigate—the rush of incoming air transformed the ember created by the porter's early-morning match into an orange flame.

He left the door ajar and the flames expanded, but still seemed manageable. Coakley searched for something in the cluttered room to smother the fire and tried to pull some canvas from the floor, but the material was tied down. Both the flames and heat grew larger and unbearable, but before seeking help, he covered the fire with a sack of charcoal, which provided temporary control.

The panicking crewman did not close the door as he left, but paused for a moment at the blower to consider whether to notify the pilothouse of the emergency—but with eighteen days on the job, he'd been repeatedly told not to bother the captain. *Got to tell the first mate. Need to find him fast!*

⊷⧲ ⧳⊶

Van Schaik admired the beautiful day through the window in the pilothouse. A soft breeze showed hope of offering some relief from this hot June day. He studied the passengers' happy faces and smiled—experience taught him that an excursion with this kind of a group on this kind of a day was all he could ever ask for. He took a deep breath and savored the moment as the ship passed Eighty-Sixth Street and approached the treacherous waters of Hell Gate.

⊷⧲ ⧳⊶

The band began another selection, "Poet and Peasant," and the stately sound of the piece matched the wonderful view of Manhattan. The engines went into high gear just as the music picked up volume. The crowd cheered as the confluence of speed and music took hold of their passions. Reverend Haas continued his walk-through in his official capacity as host and tipped his hat to the talented bandleader. Professor Maurer's daughter giggled and whispered to her mother as she noticed the pastor's gesture.

Helmut Wagner stayed by Haas's side and did his best to absorb the rever-end's style and approach with parishioners. Every time someone offered a com-pliment about the organization of the annual outing, he deflected the praise and said, "All our gratitude goes to hard-working volunteers like this young man." After the second instance of this remark, Helmut said, "My contribution was small—Gerda Heinrich should receive all the credit."

The two men smelled smoke coming up from one of the staircases near the galley. Clam chowder was on the menu, but this smell carried no hint of food.

⊷⧲ ⧳⊶

Coakley made his way to the main deck and stood on a bucket to better scrutinize the expansive space, but couldn't find the first mate, who stationed himself as a rule in the vicinity of the restaurant as each of their excursions got underway. He began to push his way through the groups of excited people, and finally came upon Flanagan providing instructions to another crew member. "The ship's afire forward, and it's making good headway. What should we do?" he asked.

"Where?"

"Coming from the lamp room."

"Follow me."

Flanagan sprang into action and led his small contingent in a sprint toward the source of the fire as the flames reached the top of the staircase. Most in the area fled the scene, but some wanted answers. *Is the boat burning? Are we in danger? Where are the life preservers? Where are the lifeboats?* The men ignored the questions and ran to the blower to inform the pilothouse. Flanagan screamed into the mouthpiece, "The ship's on fire," but didn't wait for a response. His next stop, the engine room.

⊷⊷▬◉ ◉▬⊷⊷

Bodee knew it had begun, although he couldn't say why—he turned to Walter Payne and said, "Walter, say whatever you want about what you think I'm doing, but it don't matter. Something wrong with this steamship and we need to help."

"You one crazy boy. What the hell are you talking about now? I ain't never gonna work with you again. You nothing but trouble."

"Walter, look at the crew running with the first mate."

"Not sure how you knew something going on, but you right—maybe we can help. Let's follow them." The two men dropped their mops and did their best to catch up to the rest of the crew.

⊷⊷▬◉ ◉▬⊷⊷

"Sir, we're coming up on Hell Gate. This is where the *Chester Chapin* landed on the rocks twelve hours ago. The currents are still strong."

"Yes, but we'll be fine. I'm worried more about some other vessel crossing our path—remember, keep a steady speed. Slowing down in these cross currents will be a bigger issue. Careful, gentlemen."

"Aye, aye, sir."

The blower sounded, but the message was unintelligible. "Sounds like Flanagan. Did anyone get what he said?"

"No, sir . . . another craft approaching starboard . . ."

Van Schaik instructed, "Maintain course—they won't be a problem. I need you to—"

A teenage boy interrupted his order by calling through the window, "Hey, mister, the boat is on fire!"

"Get rid of the boy—must be steam. Pay attention, men, we're entering Hell Gate."

⤙▬◐ ◑▬⤚

Flanagan ran up to the chief engineer. "We've got a fire forward and need to start the water pump."

The engineer went to work despite his grave doubts about the likely results of his actions—the *Slocum*'s hoses hadn't been used for over thirteen years.

The men rushed to the fire station thirty feet away from the raging fire and pulled down the hose from the wall—it hit the floorboards with a thud and appeared snarled in several spots. The first mate directed his men to uncoil the hose while he attempted to make the connection. Bodee and Walter straightened out the tangled mess. Every time they stretched a section, more pieces of the fabric fell to the ground. The second mate called out, "All set, sir."

Flanagan twisted the valves to start the flow of water. The sound of the "whoosh" comforted the men, but only a trickle of water emerged due to multiple choke points. The straightening began again and with the second attempt, the cheap hose exploded in five different places.

Walter ran to a nearby closet and returned with fifty feet of rubber hose, which would be able to withstand the water pressure. Bodee began uncurling it, while Flanagan tried to make the connection—the hose did not fit the coupling.

Flanagan cried, "Get to the boats!" The panic began in earnest—questions from the passengers returned: *Where are the lifeboats? Where are the life preservers?*

-*-|==|⊙ ⊙|==|-*-

"Captain, the boy is right. We've got a major fire coming up from the lower deck. The message we couldn't understand on the blower was Flanagan notifying us. What are your orders?"

Van Schaik assessed the situation as the *Slocum* arrived at Sunken Meadow, across from 110th Street, surrounded by barges, tenders, and tugs. He addressed his pilots. "Men, stay calm, we'll get through this. Man your fire posts. Hopefully, it's not too bad. I'm going down to have a look."

The music of George Maurer's Band played as the captain descended the first flight of stairs. He stopped suddenly when he neared the end of the second flight as flames shot up within a few feet of his position. The captain leaned over and peered out at the main deck, which was partially engulfed in flames. The intensity of the fire continued to be spurred on by the fresh supply of both oxygen and the flammable linseed and turpentine-slushed wood. *Why did they take so long to report this fire? Oh my God, all these women and children! The flames are about to consume the main deck. Need to move the passengers higher, away from the flames. Have to get her to shore to save the passengers. Can't fight a fire like this—never seen anything this bad in all my years at sea.*

-*-|==|⊙ ⊙|==|-*-

Juba knew her grandson was being tested and prayed at her small table with Marcus by her side. Every candle was lit—she wanted him to have the full benefit of whatever the spirits could offer. Bodee had entered her life just a few days ago, but the time they spent together was meaningful and she'd done her best to prepare him. It was all happening now and she hoped he would be up to the task.

"He's stronger than you think. I know he came here as a scared little boy, but Minetta Lane has a way of making us all toughen up real quick, Juba. Same thing happened to you and me—he'll do the right thing and be okay. Don't you worry." Marcus put his arm around Juba and joined in as they summoned the spirits once more.

Bodee wondered about his actions as he clutched his pepper shaker. *Could I have prevented this disaster by saying something? No, no one would have believed me. Did what I could, Juba, and I'm proud of everything except running scared at first. Main thing is that I came back. I'm going to help as many of these folks as I can.* Bodua, the protector, was ready to play his part in whatever was about to unfold.

CHAPTER 40

Wait 'Til She's Beached

DOZENS OF YOUNG boys and girls danced in the area in front of Professor George Maurer's makeshift bandstand and their parents stood nearby tapping their feet. The musicians began another German favorite and their leader took note of several running passengers. Maurer wondered if someone had fallen overboard, but the band played on. He spotted smoke heading his way and glanced at his wife, and the look of terror on her face made him drop his baton to the ground. Once the music came to an awkward end, Maurer heard his first cry of *fire*.

Everyone ran—most away from the fire, although some entered the flames to find loved ones. The majority, however, ran in circles. Bodee rushed to the rack of life preservers and cut them loose from their mounting. A white mist rose from the floor as the once-buoyant cork inside the vests, which long ago disintegrated into dust, formed a cloud. The formerly polite, respectable German parishioners scrambled into the mess of damaged preservers in search of one of the few still in working condition. Mothers pushed, fathers bullied, and children cried. Two women snatched opposite sides of the same preserver, and their tug-of-war created another cloud of white dust as the life jacket split in half.

Bodee ran up to the hurricane deck to help with the six lifeboats and four life rafts, which needed to be released for boarding. He joined Walter and a few other men who were trying to detach the lifeboats from their location against the side of the ship. Layers of paint and varnish had sealed the boats to the *Slocum*'s side. The two porters gave each of the men scrapers and they dug through thirteen years of touch-ups. After several minutes of frenetic digging, the men pulled together to free the critical lifesaving equipment. "We need to scrape more," Walter said. One of the German men reached into Walter's toolbox and grabbed a hammer and began to whack the point of connection between the lifeboat and the ship. Bodee uncovered the wire first and motioned to Walter, who backed away. The boats were permanently attached to the side, just like the *Grand Republic*, to avoid the clanking sound that had proven to be a nuisance. The men doing the scraping left, realizing the hopelessness of their task.

The two policemen, Tessel and Kelk, tried to maintain order on the promenade deck, but their words fell on deaf ears. Once they realized the state of the life preservers and lifeboats, they tried to create as much space as possible between the passengers and the fire. The two men herded people toward the edge. Kelk turned to his partner and said, "We have too many here now, the railing will give. None of these people can swim." The panicked guests jockeyed for position and some fell to the ground as others moved past them. The height of the mob grew as people climbed on top of their fallen neighbors. The three-foot railing appeared only a foot tall and the first cluster of frightened passengers went overboard.

In the engine room, the two engineers never received word of the failed hose and continued to man the water pump while responding to calls from the pilot-house to provide more steam. They were surrounded by flames, but never left their positions. Conklin screamed, "Hold steady. Keep giving them whatever they need. They'll come down for us once things are under control up top— should be any time now."

Reverend Haas positioned his family by the edge of the promenade deck and ushered people in the area to the relative safety of their spot. He struggled through approaching flames to try and close the sliding doors for some temporary protection. His wife pleaded with him, "George, no, no, you can't go. Stay with us—you'll never make it." The reverend's pants caught fire, but he persisted. Once at the doors, he removed his jacket and wrapped his hands in it as he attempted to slide the door. The temperature, so intense—the skin on his hands burned. The door wouldn't budge and he retreated back to his family, who quickly extinguished his burning clothing. The crowd became oversized, and he knew the railing would give, but like everyone else, Haas didn't want to jump. The prospect of survival in the water terrified the group as much as the fire.

⋄⊨⊚ ⊚⊨⋄

Bodee remained on the hurricane deck and saw the little girl from his dream in the doorway labeled *SS Slocum*. He remembered the sense of extreme light coming from the doorway in his dream and now realized the light was fire. The heat became unbearable and he feared for the girl who was on her knees praying, "Our Father who art in Heaven, hallow be thy name . . ." Bodee moved in her direction, but his feet burned through his shoes. *Need to keep going—I must save the girl.* "Hold on, little lady. I'm coming for you. Almost there."

He reached for her at the same moment a massive flame overtook her like a tidal wave. She was gone and Bodee's shirtsleeve caught on fire. He rolled on the ground to put out the flames and worked his way back to the railing, where he found Helmut, Gerda, and Eddie, who came to his aid.

⋄⊨⊚ ⊚⊨⋄

The captain and the pilots held fast in the pilothouse, which was besieged by fire. The *Slocum* was a lost cause but they hoped to buy time to save as many passengers as possible. Van Schaik maintained his composure in the midst of absolute chaos and considered his options. *I could bring her around and head back to Sunken Meadow by Hell Gate so the wind won't feed the fire and everyone will have more time aboard. This way people will have a chance in the shallow waters, but if the current takes me onto the rocks, I'll lose everyone for sure. The Bronx or Queens shore is also an option, but I run the same risk with the currents. The only safe place I know I can navigate to is North Brother*

Island, where I have a safe place to beach, but it's a mile away and I'll be feeding the fire with the wind. The instruments still showed full power in the engines. *Sunken Meadow, Bronx, Queens, or North Brother? Feed or slow the fire?*

There was no time to further analyze or continue this self-dialogue. Fifty years of experience and his gut told him what to do. He commanded his pilots, "Put her on North Brother Island."

⊶ ⊷

The sight of the burning steamer did not go unnoticed and several boats of various types navigated toward the fast-moving inferno. Deliveries, tours, or whatever their business—it was put aside—they were in this together and the surrounding vessels planned to do whatever they could to assist. Some fell into the wake of the *Slocum* and followed. A few stopped to pick up some of the early jumpers who survived their leap. The choice of stopping or proceeding was a difficult one and each of the captains made their own individual decisions. A calamity of this magnitude affected everyone and every vessel would help, but each decided on the role they would play.

Two prisoners and a doctor, all part of a prison workhouse program on Rikers Island, cast off in a rowboat similar to the *Slocum*'s lifeboats and headed toward the obvious destination of the burning steamship, North Brother Island. Their boat lacked speed and power, but their determination was strong. The prisoners rowed and the doctor provided navigation. They weren't sure what they would be able to do, but whatever their role might be would be evident within minutes. The two men leaned into their oars and the small craft made good headway.

⊶ ⊷

Tugboat Captain Jack Wade, of the harbor tug *John Wade*, spotted the *Slocum* and moved in her direction. He called to his pilot, "Full throttle ahead." The tug moved toward the *Slocum* and the captain estimated that two-thirds of the steamship was engulfed in fire. Hordes of people jumped into the water and others ran with no apparent purpose on the decks in the midst of flames that, in some cases, measured thirty feet in length. His decision was clear—the *John Wade* maneuvered like few other boats of its size and could approach the steamship once in shallow water. The tug only needed four feet of water to operate. The pilot slowed down as the *Slocum* passed and fell into its wake along with several other boats. Wade barked, "Keep some distance, and wait 'til she's beached."

C H A P T E R 41

Overboard

MICHAEL MCGRANN, THE steward in charge of the ship's cash, held out as long as he could in his back office. He worried about any diversion that might be used to steal the significant sum of money the *Slocum* had on hand. Frank Barnaby, the president of the company, had told him that should the ship ever be robbed, he would be out of a job. With a wife and children, McGrann was determined for this fate not to befall him.

He filled a large bag with a substantial amount of coins and bills and placed it inside a sack, in an effort to make it somewhat waterproof. Even though he was a strong swimmer, McGrann understood the additional weight would make things more difficult, so he strapped on his own personal life preserver he'd taken from the rack months ago, ran directly for the railing, and leaped, holding the double-bagged money over his shoulder.

McGrann didn't realize the cork inside his life jacket had long since disintegrated. The good condition of the exterior canvas fooled him into believing this was one of the better life jackets. The net effect of water absorbing cork dust, along with the heavy coins, meant he jumped carrying another fifty pounds. He hit the water and sunk quickly; he was determined to hold onto the money as he attempted to resurface, but such a feat was impossible. Eventually, he released his grasp on the bag and found his way to the surface, but the exhaustion from the climb proved to be too much. After taking a few breaths of air, he sunk again for the last time.

⊷═◉ ◉═⊷

George Maurer guarded his location by the railing where he stood with his family. Whenever jumpers came too close, he pushed them to the side so their forward momentum would not inadvertently knock any of his family overboard. He watched each set of two and three leap together and observed what initially happened in the water. Many of those wearing the ship's life preservers never resurfaced and the people who did were often driven back down by others who collided with them as they jumped a few seconds later.

He gave his family their instructions, "Okay, we're not using these life preservers. The only ones left are old and drag you down rather than keep you up. Our trick will be to leap when no one else will immediately follow us. So we'll wait for a break and then we'll go. Move away after you resurface to avoid being struck by other people. Do you understand?"

Margaret Maurer countered, "Oh, George, I can't do this. I'll take my chances up here. Someone must be coming soon to help us."

"Not an option, honey—we all go or we all stay. I'm the head of this family and in my opinion, if we stay, we die. You're probably worried that when you jump, you won't be able to come back up. Don't worry, I've got an idea." George left momentarily and returned to his family with a long stretch of rope that he attached to his wife's waist. He said, "When the time is right, we'll lower you down into the water. This way you won't sink low like you would if you jumped. Remember, as soon as you come up in the water, move further out because Clara, Matilda, and I will be jumping right away or someone else might, and we don't want you to be hurt."

"George, I don't know about this. I'm not sure I can do this . . ."

"Yes, you can. No more talk. The time is right, now." The bandleader tied the other end of the rope around himself and began lowering her down. Luckily, no other jumpers appeared and Margaret Maurer moved away after resurfacing. George whispered to his daughters, "Let's wait for this family to jump first," as a father approached with his two boys. They moved about ten feet away, and the bandleader took each of his daughter's hands and said, "On the count of three. One, two, three."

They surfaced together and smiled, but the family who witnessed their jump decided to imitate their approach and moved to the same departure point, counted to three, and leaped with their hands clasped. Margaret Maurer screamed, "Over here!" just as her family was crushed before her eyes.

⊷▬● ●▬⊶

The captain had North Brother's Island within his sight, but the nearby pier in the Bronx beckoned. He glanced again in both directions, and looked to his pilot, who did the same thing. *Never like to reverse a command. Often it isn't what you do, but simply how well you stick to your plan that makes the difference . . . but the Bronx shore is so close—we can be at the pier in seconds.* "Bring her to the Bronx." The pilot expected the change in plans and swung toward the shore.

Bodee sat with Gerda, Eddie, and Helmut at the edge of the hurricane deck. The three adults planned their next move while Eddie sat on the floor, holding onto Bodee's right leg. The abrupt turn knocked Helmut and Gerda, along with dozens of other passengers, over the railing. The weight of Eddie on Bodee's leg was of some assistance in grounding him as he reached out to help his friends— he could only grab Gerda's hand. Helmut banged his head on the rail before falling into the river in an unconscious state.

Bodee called out, "I got you," and Eddie pulled on his pant leg, saying, "And I got you."

Bodee maneuvered Gerda back aboard just before another sharp course correction from the pilothouse reverted to their original destination. "Helmut, oh my God, what happened to Helmut?" Gerda cried out. "We must do something. It can't end like this for him. He's such a good man." Gerda dropped to the ground as she continued to cry repeatedly, "He's such a good man."

Bodee gave her a chance to regroup, but the flames were advancing and it was time for them to make their exit. "Ms. Gerda, Helmut was my friend too," Bodee said. "Now we just met, but I think people know when they meet someone true who'll be their friend for years to come and that's how I felt about him and I hope he felt the same way about me. I don't want to get your hopes up, though, because this bloodstain on the railing is from him—he hit his head on the way overboard. I don't think Helmut survived."

"Oh my God, he was so full of promise."

"Yes, he told me his dream was to become a minister and I have no doubt he would have achieved it, but he would have wanted us to get through this, so I need you to listen to me."

"Yes, you're right. What do you want us to do?"

"We'll leap when no one else does—the flames are almost on us and all of these sudden shifts in direction make me worry the captain doesn't have a plan.

The two of you go first and when you come up, I want you to do something called the dog paddle." Bodee moved his arms and legs in a circular motion. "This will keep you afloat. I'll dive over you and you swim toward me. Don't worry, do what I showed you. Shoes off, both of you, and loosen your clothes—you need to be able to move."

Bodee waited for two groups of three to clear the area and he moved ten feet away before giving the signal. The two went over, barefoot and hand-in-hand. After coming up to the surface, they began to dog paddle away from the ship. He removed his own shoes and backed up as far as he could without encountering flames and took a running start toward the ledge. The men in the lifeboat from Rikers Island and the crew from the *John Wade* witnessed it, as did many of the other vessels trailing the *Slocum*. His running start and athletic headfirst dive created an arc similar to a bird swooping in for a landing, which he did with a perfect entry into the water about fifteen feet beyond Gerda and Eddie. He cried, "Over here. Over here."

⊷⊨▬◉ ◉▬⊫⊶

The Haas family never intended to jump and hoped to survive onboard until help arrived when they docked. The constant changes in direction, however, made them doubt any firm destination was set and the reverend turned his back to the flames to discuss options with his family—he saw it in his daughter's eyes first. A mob of ten emerged from the flames and desperately sought the relief that only water could provide—they charged the Haas family in a straight line, holding hands, and the entire cluster of people fell into the water in a tangled mess. Somehow, the Haases maintained their grip on each other and reached the surface of the water at about the same time. Both mother and daughter struggled to stay afloat. The next collection of flaming passengers rained directly on the Haas family and the minister resurfaced, but his family was gone.

⊷⊨▬◉ ◉▬⊫⊶

"Doctor Lewis, over there. I see some survivors," John Grover, one of the prisoners aboard the lifeboat, called out.

"Yes, let's try to take them aboard."

Grover and fellow inmate Frank Arnold pivoted toward the obviously struggling group. The doctor offered encouragement, "Put your backs into it, boys!"

⇥ ⇤

The fire, now being fed by unlimited oxygen, engulfed the boat. A few pockets of people remained in some isolated areas that had escaped the blaze. The *Slocum* approached North Brother Island and Van Schaik tried to maneuver as close to the beach as possible. The pilots heard two crashes back-to-back and rushed to the windows to determine the cause.

"Captain, the bulkheads must have given out. A portion of the promenade deck collapsed."

"Yes, I see it also. The second crash must have been the rocks. We've arrived—I'm guessing we're about twenty feet away from the beach. Let's see who we can help."

CHAPTER 42

Damn the Tug!

THE *MASSASOIT*, A one hundred-fifty-three-foot prisoner transport vessel operated by the Department of Correction, approached the *Slocum*'s location on the rocks. The captain assessed the situation with his pilots, "Okay, boys, I figure she's resting in about six feet of water at its bow and around twenty at the stern, so we're not going to be able to come so close—loads of survivors are right in front of us. We'll hold up here."

A crew member launched one of the *Massasoit*'s lifeboats and rowed toward a group of people close to the inferno while his crewmates sprayed the fire hose over his head to provide some level of cooling. Seven desperate passengers swarmed the rowboat and quickly boarded. The deckhand headed back to the ship.

The *John Wade* was the only craft able to navigate into the shallow waters by the bow of the *Slocum* because of the small amount of water she displaced. The windows shattered and the old girl groaned as she neared the steamer. The pilot warned, "We'll lose her!" The captain countered, "Damn the tug! Let her burn! Wait . . . straightaway!"

A mass of people crowded into a corner came into view. Reverend George Schultze and the Sunday school teacher, Mr. Muller, stood between advancing flames and fifty children they had rounded up.

Schultze knew the children had no chance in the water and peered at the sky, "Please Lord, deliver these boys and girls to safety." One of the older boys pointed behind him and Schultze turned expecting to encounter the flame that would mark the end of this horrendous experience, but instead he found the *Wade* making its approach.

The giant of a man provided an excellent target as he waved his burned arms. The youngsters stood and shouted, "Over here!" The tugboat was on fire, but not about to turn back. The two men loaded the youths one by one and Schultze, the last to board, glanced up and whispered, "Thank you," as he checked one last time for anyone else.

Others made their way to the tug, including the two hired policemen, Van Tessel and Kelk, who distinguished themselves with their courage in fighting the fire. Edward Flanagan bounded onto the tug screaming, "She's gonna explode. Got to leave." The crew ignored his pleas and he tried to disengage the line to force the *Wade*'s departure. The enraged captain threw Flanagan overboard. Officer Kelk offered the disgraced first mate a parting thought, "You fucking coward, you're on your own."

"He's right, we need to leave right away," the pilot said. Wade hesitated, but agreed. The boat, however, would not cooperate. A line became caught in the propeller and the crew fought the fire as they worked to remove the ensnared rope.

The *Zophar Mills* came upon the scene and reacted to the flames by redirecting its fire hoses from the *Slocum* onto the *Wade*. In the meanwhile, another ship attached a line to the tug as more people leaped onboard. Within seconds, the tugboat was pulled out of the danger zone. Captain Jack Wade took stock of his achievement—one hundred and fifty-five people rescued.

CHAPTER 43

The Vision Unfolds

BODEE SHOUTED TO Gerda and Eddie, "Over here! Over here!" The dog paddle, effective at staying afloat, was not known for forward progress. He turned sideways to take his first stroke in their direction and was pulled on the leg from below in separate directions. Pain shot up through his spine as he headed underwater. He bent over at the waist and found two women grasping his legs and starting to claw their way up his torso. *Got to get loose or we're all gonna die.*

Someone took hold of him from behind and he fell back, but the women held on. *Got no choice.* He elbowed the person at his back and removed the two women clawing at his legs with a combination of knees and punches. He noted a look of peace on their faces as they each reached the breaking point. The lack of oxygen for an extended period of time triggered an involuntary attempt at breathing—their lungs filled with water and they floated away with an eerie sense of tranquility.

He hurried to the top and cried, "Hang on, I'm coming." Eddie continued to dog paddle, but Gerda vanished. Bodee didn't know if she suffered from fatigue or if she'd been pulled below by another victim, so he swam to her last location and dove straight down.

Must be twenty people down here. He worked through the jumbled humanity and brushed aside the floating hats, high heels, and garments. Some of those down below had died, but others were fighting to hold on. Three women grabbed him and pulled him into a tangle with two small boys, one in a blue shirt who showed no signs of life and one with a brown shirt, who kicked and scratched as much as the women. Bodee tried not to strike back, but he needed to break free. *Can't stay down much longer. Got to pick one of these folks to save and head to the surface.*

He grabbed the boy with the brown shirt, extracted himself from the deadly web, and pushed away from the pack with the boy in tow. Bodee began to head to the surface, but stopped when he spotted Gerda's lifeless body sinking right in front of him. He looked at Gerda and then at the boy, and realized he had grabbed the one with the blue shirt. He looked back at the pack and saw the child with the brown shirt waving his arms. *Can't save them both—don't think I can go back. Got to decide. I'll save Mrs. Gerda.* He snatched her by the back of her collar and rushed to the surface, resting her on her back facing the sky. After some time, she coughed up water. *She's alive.*

The Rikers crew pulled up, and the man with the oar from his dream helped Gerda into the rowboat, where she joined another five people. She sat up and said, "You got to find my boy, can't lose another one."

On his first dive, he found a man who appeared ready to take his last deadly breath. Bodee brought him to the top and over to the lifeboat, where the number of occupants was close to the maximum. One of the first people saved by the Rikers Island trio said, "Enough, we can't hold any more." The two inmates stared into his eyes and he backed down.

Bodee returned to Eddie's last location. The doctor directed the men to move closer in order to pull the next few saves on board. The boat was at capacity and Bodee had no energy left, but he promised to find Eddie. "Come up to rest for a minute," the doctor said.

The complaining passenger countered, "We ain't got no space for some Darkey. Let him go off on his own." The two prisoners stood—the implication clear, but all to no end because Bodee's job wasn't done. He muttered, "Got to find him," and went back to work.

Bodee went down again, and again, and again. He saved nine people, one at a time, and repeated the line, "Got to find him," before plunging back in. On his last dive, he stayed under too long and Gerda turned to the doctor, "Someone needs to check on him, he's—"

One of the survivors pointed as he came up for air some distance away. The doctor called out, "You done all you can do—we'll come to you. Stay put."

Gerda bawled, "No. No. He's got to find my boy. Please help him. He can't do this all alone."

Bodee's arms were like rubber and he screamed, "Got to find him. Got to find him," and then he detected a little head about fifty feet away. *My God, there he is.* After a few strokes in Eddie's direction, extreme fatigue set in and he stopped to tread water and conserve energy. *Need your help, Juba, need to be strong. Must rest my arms.* He flipped over and backpedaled for what seemed like an eternity. *Must be almost there. Why is it getting so hot?* Bodee righted himself to investigate and spotted Eddie dog paddling with sweat pouring down his face less than thirty yards from the flaming shell of the *Slocum. Need to get him out—not safe here.*

The doctor assessed the situation. "Too dangerous to go so near the burning steamer. Let's give him a chance to bring the boy back."

"No, you must help him. He's so tired. That's my son! You must help both of them!"

"Ma'am, I can't risk everyone's life for your boy. This Bodee did more than anyone could be expected to do. Don't understand where he finds the strength, he's built like a toothpick, but I've got faith in him."

The return trip seemed impossible and the weight of the water kept pushing Bodee down. *Got to find the power, Juba. Please help me.* The doctor instructed the men to travel a small stretch of the way toward their last two passengers. Bodee sank again and wasn't sure if he could climb back to the top. He looked at Eddie, who made his dog paddle motion, and somehow found the strength. Once at the surface he cried, "Over here. Over here," and waved with his left arm, which caused him to sink, yet again. Finally, someone in the small boat called out, "Hang on, we're close."

Bodee couldn't continue, but gave Eddie one final push, which provided enough momentum to reach the safety of Gerda's arms. "My baby, I thought you were gone. Thank God you're safe."

I did it. I saved Eddie, Bodee thought. *I just need the oar. Please let me see the oar.* A massive wave engulfed him, and he sank, but just like the dream, the boat moved toward him as his head went under.

The doctor extended the oar into the water and screamed, "Grab on." Bodee took hold of the end. *Thank you, Lord. I made it!*

The tug came from below—someone latched onto his right ankle, which made him lose his grip. He went down without taking a last breath of air. The lack of oxygen didn't cause the fatal last gasp that would fill his lungs with water—he simply lost consciousness without ingesting a drop. A peaceful smile came over his face as he clutched his pepper shaker in his right hand. Bodua had lived up to his name and hadn't cut and run. *Juba will be proud of me.*

The survivors in the rowboat searched for a sign of their savior, but he was gone from sight. Gerda and Eddie knelt by the side and offered a prayer just as the *General Slocum* exploded, scattering the water with debris. The doctor ordered the men to the shore.

CHAPTER 44

North Brother Island

THE RIVERSIDE HOSPITAL for Contagious Diseases on North Brother Island served several hundred patients with a staff of one hundred-sixty-four, including thirty-five nurses and six physicians. Screams of "Steamer afire" echoed throughout the facility as the highly trained personnel learned of the disaster and split into groups. The largest contingent made their way to the beach, where they created a fire battalion atop the seawall, which overlooked the sand. The other group headed for the river. Dozens were pulled from the shallow water, which still presented a challenge to the passengers of the *Slocum*, who had no concept of swimming. The workers encouraged those still aboard the burning ship to jump. Once all of the live victims were safely ashore, the second group began rounding up the floating corpses.

The medical team prioritized their work by attempting to revive the lifeless before addressing the issues of the conscious. First, they laid the individual on their back with their arms stretched above their head and pulled their arms down sharply to the side. This movement was repeated several times. Next, the victim was bent over one of the worker's legs, while a nurse or doctor pushed on their back. The objective of both steps—to expel water from the lungs—was only achieved in a handful of cases.

Reverend Haas received the treatment and the pushing on his back in step two revived him. "Where is my family? Did they make it?" he asked.

The answer: "We just don't know."

By 10:45 a.m., no further efforts were made to resuscitate the unresponsive and attention turned to the conscious. The employees provided blankets and whiskey to all and applied bandages to those who had battled in the desperate underwater fights. Significant numbers of nurses and doctors made their way over from Manhattan and supplemented the efforts of the forty or so medical professionals. In addition, a large contingent of policemen maintained order while helping to move the deceased onto the lawn in front of the main building.

At 10:55, the skeleton of the *Slocum* was raised by the incoming tide, which caused her to be set adrift. Fires actively burned in the wreckage and this posed a hazard to other vessels. Several tugs attached lines to the debris and escorted the formerly grand ship to its next resting place in the harbor in Hunts Point, where she sunk and generated a stream of smoke that lasted for hours.

Once the steamship moved off the beach, bodies trapped underneath floated ashore, adding to the ranks of the dead and the operation transitioned from rescue to recovery. By 11:15 a.m., the remains of one hundred-fifty parishioners rested in an orderly line with the assumption that many more remained at sea.

Photographers and reporters roamed the grounds, taking pictures and interviewing survivors with the aim of being the first to report the story. *The New York World* won this competition with its special edition, which hit newsstands at 11:30 a.m. with the headline, "Horror on the East River. Hundreds Feared Dead."

George Haas walked through the rows on the lawn with the agonizing goal of looking for something he didn't want to find—his wife, daughter, sister, and nephew. He consoled those who walked with him, searching for their own family. No member of the Haas family lay among the dead, but he did make two upsetting discoveries—Helmut Wagner on his back with a massive gash across his forehead and bandleader George Maurer with an imprint of a large boot on the side of his face. The minister paused often to offer prayers, but devoted extra time to his young volunteer, who would never get the chance to live a full life in the church. He held Helmut's hand and whispered, "You would have made an excellent reverend."

Frank Barnaby, the president of the Knickerbocker Steamship Company, sent a lineup of top executives to assess the situation. Their official reason for being there was to provide help and assistance, but their true purpose was to keep the senior crew away from the authorities and get them back to the office to craft and coordinate their stories. Barnaby had already asked his bookkeeper to correct an *error* in the books related to the failure to record the purchase of safety equipment, and she had complied.

The company men grasped the enormity of the loss of life as soon as they arrived and understood the estimate of two hundred or so dead grossly miscalculated the magnitude of the tragedy. The *Slocum*'s passenger list included thirteen hundred names and they realized that rather than count the dead and assume there might be more, it would be more accurate to tally the survivors and add a few more to that number. By their estimates, as many as one thousand people might have perished in the terrible fire.

The Knickerbocker men located and shipped off several of the crew within minutes of their arrival, but took a while to locate Captain Van Schaik and his two pilots, who had snuck away. They were later intercepted by police and brought to the station for questioning.

Given that the facility on North Brother Island served a population with transmittable diseases, the hospital administration didn't admit anyone who needed additional attention. Those victims were taken to the Bronx by boat and then admitted to hospitals on the mainland. Haas collapsed again after discovering Helmut Wagner and George Maurer, and was taken to Lincoln Hospital in the Bronx.

Other people were given first aid before being taken to the mainland and placed on the elevated train for a ride home to Little Germany. Many boarded missing shirts, shoes, socks, and portions of dresses, but what they missed the most were their loved ones.

CHAPTER 45

Where is He?

WORD ARRIVED AT the *Grand Republic* through Captain Pease, who gathered the men together for the announcement. "Men, we received some disturbing information about the *General Slocum*—we lost her. She went up in flames on the East River and went aground on North Brother Island. Many people died, but the entire crew survived—the employee list shows everyone accounted for. The bosses fear hundreds may be dead and Mr. Barnaby himself identified the cause of the fire—someone tossed a match on some bananas left on the deck. Our men did their best to fight the blaze."

One of the men raised his hand. "Sir, I always worried about the fire gear on the *Republic* and the *Slocum*. Did it work?"

"Mr. Barnaby assured me that all of our hoses and preservers worked perfectly and the men fought the fire in a most courageous way. Just as a precaution, though, Mr. Barnaby wants us all to be as prepared as possible, so stop what you're doing today and toss all of our old stuff in these bins. By the end of the week, the new replacement materials will be here. Like I said, after something like this happens, they're giving us the best."

Pease walked away and First Mate Gilbride called into a tight huddle the ten men who came in on their day off. "The fire equipment isn't worth shit and this might have been us, but at least we'll be safe now. He gave you the official story to repeat if you want to hold on to your jobs, but those life preservers and hoses haven't been used for years. Remember, if you want to keep working, you can grumble to each other, but if anybody asks anything, you say what Pease said. Understand?"

The men all said together, "Yes, Mr. Gilbride."

Duane stayed back to review the listing. After scanning the sheet, he raised his head and asked, "Where's Bodee's name? We sent him to the *Slocum* for the day."

"Remember, he never completed his papers, so he didn't officially exist, but if everyone else is okay, I'm sure he's fine."

"Yeah, I guess you're right."

"Don't worry, we should see him first thing in the morning."

⊸▮⊛ ⊛▮⊸

The *Tribune* didn't run the story first, but they featured the first pictures. The newsies lined up to receive their extra stacks.

"Listen up, boys, this issue is about a massive fire on the water. The headline says, *Inferno on the River.*"

Two-Tooth Tommy interrupted, "What's an inferno?"

"A really serious fire. That's easy enough. Right, Two-Tooth?"

"Yeah, yeah, let me see the picture."

"You can look all you want once you buy your papers."

He handed over fifty cents, studied the image, and called out, "Hey, what's the name of the boat?"

"The *General Slocum.*"

Tommy threw his stack to the ground, dashed out of the warehouse, and made his way over to Little Germany to check on Triple N.

⊸▮⊛ ⊛▮⊸

Juba released Marcus's hand and said, "Everything is over, and I'm not so sure things turned out like they supposed to. My grandson tried, but things don't feel right. Marcus, you got to go find out what you can. He told me he needed to report to the East Third Street Pier."

"Okay, but you should eat something and rest—been sitting at this here table too long. Be back soon."

Marcus headed out, but not directly for the docks. *Silvy will know what to do.*

⊷▬◉ ◉▬⊶

"Need your help. Got to figure out what happened to Bodee—he reported for work at the East Side piers, and something real bad happened today, but we're not sure what. Juba felt something—need to find out."

Silvy's heart fell, and he reached into his pile of newspapers and picked out the one marked special edition because he remembered the newsie screaming, "Fire on the East River." He held up the front page photograph. "What's the name of his steamer?"

"Not sure."

"All right, I hope this story will tell us something. *The SS General Slocum, one of the premier vessels of the Knickerbocker Steamship Company, left the East Side docks this morning filled with parishioners from the St. Mark's Lutheran Church expecting a day of fun and games. By the time the Slocum reached upper Manhattan, the steamer was engulfed in flames. The source of the fire isn't known at this time, but hundreds are feared dead. The Slocum came to a final stop on North Brother's Island off the shore of the Bronx. Survivors were sent home to Little Germany via the elevated line.*"

"Enough, he works for Knickerbocker and this ship left from the East Side. This got to be the one. You finish up reading and come on over to Juba's place when you're done."

⊷▬◉ ◉▬⊶

Tommy sat on the stoop of Gerda Heinrich's building. He knocked on every door and no one spoke to him, at least in English, but everyone cried. All he could do was wait. The parade of people began around 4 p.m., when some of the folks who were dressed so handsomely a few short hours ago emerged from the train in tattered and missing clothes. Parents ran to meet sons and daughters, only to find out they no longer had children. Husbands rushed to find wives and discovered they no longer had spouses. Few families remained intact—Little Germany was devastated.

Tommy waited as six different groups came down the steps from the subway. *Where is he?*

⋯⊷ ⊶⋯

Dieter Wagner went to St. Mark's hoping for word about Helmut. He went over his logic one more time. *Yes, Helmut would first go to the church to see how he could help. This is where I need to be. Also, Reverend Haas's son has a telephone and he received a message that his father was okay. I'll ask him if he can give me information about my boy.*

"Show me once more, how can this list still be only one page long? Why don't you know who is okay? Let me speak to the reverend's son. Please, he can make a call."

"So sorry, sir," the volunteer said. "He isn't available and this is all we can tell you."

Dieter returned to the pew closest to the office, clutching the shoe polish he bought earlier to save his son the trouble. He traced the outline of the small tin can as tears streamed down his face. The young man came out of the office with a new list to post on the wall. Dozens crammed around him to for another look—the document still only one page. The volunteer sensed the impatience of the group and called out, "Two new additions, Matilda Goosen and Roger Schmidt." Dieter thought, *Where is he?*

⋯⊷ ⊶⋯

After disposing of all of the decrepit life preservers, the day's work was done. Duane reached into his pocket and pulled out Bodee's address. *I remember him saying he lived in a real rough neighborhood—I'll take this for protection.* He picked up a short section of pipe he found in the lamp room and began his walk to the Bend.

He paused at the corner of Sixth Avenue and Minetta, grabbed onto his tube, and proceeded to talk out loud, "I'm a friend of Bodee Rivers. Don't want no problem." Three of Blood's men came out from the shadows and moved toward Duane, who slightly spread his feet and prepared for battle.

"What you gonna do with your little pipe?" Blade asked as he whipped out his switchblade.

"Don't want no fuss, just lookin' for Bodee is all."

Blade laughed. "We're having a little fun with you. If you a friend of his, you got protection. Walk toward the man in the black hat across the street." He pointed to Juba's building, where Blood stood in front.

"Who you?"

"I'm Duane and I work with Bodee. Don't want no trouble."

"Stop making all that fuss. No one gonna hurt you. Is Bodee okay? Was he on the ship that went on fire today?"

"Yes, but I don't know what happened to him. This is why I'm here. Thought he might be home."

"Ain't back yet. I'm his uncle and his grandma upstairs."

Marcus brought him into the living area, where Juba sat with Silvy. "His name Duane, and he works with Bodee."

"What you got to say to us about my grandson?"

"Well, ma'am, we got word about the fire a few hours ago. The crew all made it, but I'm not sure about Bodee, though, because he's not listed with the rest."

"What do you mean?"

"I mean his name might be left off because he started the other day and didn't do all of the payroll paperwork yet, so he didn't really exist."

"So, he's okay?" Marcus asked.

"Not sure."

Juba began her guttural moan, but this didn't lead to invoking spirits or any of her other religious rituals—it just gradually petered out and led to tears, along with one basic question, "Where is he?"

Chapter 46

The East 23rd Street Pier

THE POLICE AND coroner's departments labored together to establish a temporary morgue at the East Twenty-Third Street Pier. Officers placed the bodies on beds of ice and lined them up in neat rows. The scene from the lawn on North Brother Island cycled in an endless loop as people walked the aisles hoping not to find what they were looking for. Most of the bodies were charred beyond recognition, but loved ones identified many from clothing or jewelry. The authorities did their best to maintain order, but Gerda Heinrich understood her role—as one of the lucky few survivors, she needed to help.

The crowd gathered outside as if they were waiting for a sold-out show, and the police did their best to allow waves of people to enter in order to avoid overcrowding. Gerda began mingling through the crowd and came across Ronald Mueller, who found his wife clutching their five-year-old daughter in her arms. *What do I say?* Instinctively, she realized words weren't the answer and offered a shoulder to cry on and a heartfelt pat on the back.

Gerda continued her slow walk up the aisle and fell to her knees when she came upon her dear Helmut. She sobbed and broke down on the floor in tears. Ronald Mueller walked to her side and offered his handkerchief and helped her to her feet. They both hugged and went their separate ways.

The crowd thinned at around 7 p.m. and Gerda noticed Tommy against the far wall. She waved him over.

"Where is he, where's Eddie, is he okay?" Tommy asked. "I shouldn't have let him go! You don't understand, I'm supposed to take care of him and I let him down. Is he all right? Tell me!"

"Eddie is back at my apartment—he's fine."

Tommy threw is hat in the air and screamed, "Woo hoo!" His celebration was misplaced amid all of the overwhelming grief, but she hugged and escorted him toward the door. "How about we go home and say hello to Eddie, and you'll have some dinner with us. Okay?"

He presented both of his signature teeth as a response and asked, "You got pork 'n' beans?"

"Anything is possible."

Juba returned to her small table and sat quietly, holding her saltshaker. She didn't feel much energy at all related to her typically intense connection with her grandson. Her worst fears rushed through her mind. *Made so many mistakes with him . . . shouldn't have encouraged him with all my talk about Bodua, the protector, and I should have questioned the way he read the vision. So sorry, Akua, you were right to keep me away.* Tears streamed down her face. *Got to go tell Nellie.*

"Walter, glad you're okay—what a terrible thing."

"Like nothing I ever seen, Duane. She went up in flames in minutes. The damn fire hoses didn't work at all and I'm happy I jumped off when I did. The Germans . . . none of them can swim at all and they all drowned. This was the most horrible thing—women, children—the looks on their faces . . . they'll be in my head for a long time."

"Can't tell you I understand and I hope I never do. All the crew got off okay?"

"Yeah, I think we all did. At least that's what Barnaby says. Didn't see everybody with my own eyes, though, because they rounded us up in small bunches to tell us to say the fire started with a match and some bananas. Lots of bullshit, the life preservers were for shit—watch out for yourself on the *Republic.*"

"Don't think we going out again anytime soon and no matter to me because I plan to find another line of work. Is Bodee okay?"

"I think so. One of the men said he's a hero—saved a bunch of people by pulling them out from under and taking them to a rowboat. He's a real strong swimmer and didn't show no fear, but those daydreams you warned me about are more than that—he's kind of a scary guy. He knew what was gonna happen. Didn't understand how."

"What do you mean?"

"Well, he acted odd from the moment he came aboard. Next thing, he got off, came back, and then I gave him a piece of my mind because he didn't work at all. That's when he told me the *Slocum* was in trouble. I didn't tell anyone about him knowing because they'll want to blame someone. Looked for him after we all got to North Brother Island to tell him to keep his mouth shut—they'd love to put this on a Black man. Truth doesn't mean a thing to Knickerbocker, they looking for the best lie."

"Yeah, I understand, but I want to find him. You think he went to North Brother?"

"Probably at first, but everyone gone by now, even the people who got injured. They sent most of the German people home on the trains. You have his address?"

"Yeah, already checked his place. Nobody seen him and they worried too. His grandma got the same kind of *I know what's gonna happen* stuff going on."

"Must run in the family."

"This a different type of family. The uncle scares the shit out of me."

"Okay, if he got hurt, they wouldn't take a Black man to one of the Manhattan hospitals, but Bronx Lebanon Hospital treats Blacks. Remember, tell him not to say a word. He's not on the roster for the crew because they didn't want to pay him for his first few days—this means he wasn't even officially on board. Better for him to stay quiet."

"I think you're right and I'll tell him so when I find him. I'll check Bronx Lebanon."

"Okay, Duane, he's an odd one, but I liked him even though he was the worst damn worker, ever! Let me know when he turns up."

"Will do."

⤜◉ ◉⤛

"Nellie, sorry for busting in here like this. Got to talk to you about Bodee."

"Is he okay? We planning to go out on Friday."

"He's in trouble. You heard about the boat that burned up on the river today?"

"Yeah, not Bodee's steamer, though. He's on the *Grand Republic*."

"Those two steamships are owned by the same company he works for and they loaned him for the day. He never came home and someone from the *Republic* came over looking for him a little while ago. Things don't feel right and I'm worried."

"He'll be okay because he swims so well. This is the way we got to think." Nellie grabbed Juba's hands. "Let's go back to your place. I want to wait with you. Let me tell Mama."

Juba felt something and pulled away from Nellie. "We'll learn something at sundown, not saying tomorrow for sure, but one day soon, we'll have our answer. You welcome to stay with me for as long as you want."

"I'll pack a bag and be right back."

C H A P T E R 47

The Hospitals

Duane made his way down Westchester Avenue to Bronx Lebanon. He entered and asked about victims of the *Slocum* disaster, but answers didn't come quickly, so he rested against the wall opposite the visitor's desk. The all-White staff and clientele offered a collection of stares and smiles—it wasn't clear if Blacks were welcome, so he kept as low a profile as possible. The nurse called him over.

"What's the name of the person you're here for?"

"Bodee Rivers."

"What kind of German name is that?"

"No kind at all, because he ain't no German—he a Black man."

"I think you're confused. The *General Slocum* carried parishioners from St. Mark's, a German church in downtown Manhattan. No Black people at all."

"Not a passenger—he crew." *Damn, Walter told me not to admit Bodee worked on the Slocum. I made a mistake.*

"No crew came to Bronx Lebanon and most of the injured passengers went to facilities in Manhattan. We got the ones who only needed a little attention and they took the train home after being discharged. Never treated any Coloreds."

"I checked his house and they ain't seen him since he left work this morning."

"Well, if he started out on North Brother Island, the hospital has him in their records with a note about where he went next. One more ferry goes out tonight and the dock isn't far from here on 132nd Street."

"I'll go check—worried about him and I promised his family I'd try to locate him."

"Okay, hurry up, you don't want to miss your ride!"

He rushed toward 132nd Street with a combination of walking and running, and arrived as the final passenger boarded.

"All aboard. Wait, Joe, we got one more."

⋅►▬◐ ◑▬◄⋅

Ain't so hard to figure out where to go, Duane thought as he walked toward the entrance to the Riverside Hospital for Contagious Disease, the only building of substance within view. The last group of police prepared to depart on the same boat he arrived in. One of the workers called out to him, "Hey you, yeah, you, either you come right back on or you're stuck here for the night."

"Stuck here for the night? I only need a little time to ask about someone. Can't you give me a couple of minutes?"

"Listen, all these nurses and policemen are waiting to go back to the Bronx. No way I'm gonna hold them up for a Darkey. We leave in three minutes."

A policeman asked, "Who you looking for?"

"Bodee Rivers."

"Never here. I worked with the list of everyone we sent to the morgue or hospitals on the mainland and every single one was a German name. Ask inside, if you want, but you're wasting your time."

"We're pushing off—staying or going?" the pilot asked.

"Didn't come all this way to run off without being sure. You go ahead, I'm going inside."

"Suit yourself, the next boat docks at six a.m. and heads back at six fifteen a.m."

Duane headed into the building and found no reception desk. A maintenance worker emptying a garbage can noticed his surprise. "Yeah, not many visitors here—you may be our first Colored visitor ever. My name is Nelson and this is the place where they put people with diseases others can catch. Lots of tuberculosis, typhus, things like that. Who you looking for?"

"I'm looking for one of the people from the *Slocum*."

"All those people are gone. Might be some information at the nurses' station, though. What's the person's name?"

"Bodee Rivers, and yes, I know it doesn't sound German. At least that's what everyone keeps telling me."

"What he look like?"

"He's a tall, thin Black man, about twenty years old."

"Well, I came in after all of the craziness with the dead bodies and survivors, but I don't think we had any Colored people in the whole bunch of them."

"That's what I thought, but I wanted to check. Now I missed the last boat back to the Bronx."

"Yeah, next one is in the morning, but I can set you up in a place with a real soft chair. You need to stay out of the way around here. Remember, this is the hospital with all of the 'catchy' diseases. You don't want to go back home with anything more than you came with. Understand?"

"Yeah, show me where this chair is."

Nelson laughed. "You're standing right next to it!" He nodded in the direction of a rickety wooden chair—the only one in sight.

"Yeah, *real soft*, like you said."

"Remember, don't wander around. I'll try to bring you back a little food on my break."

"Thanks."

Duane sat and thought about the craziness of his day. *Why am I doing all this for someone I just started working with?* He shifted his weight in an effort to find a comfortable way to sit on the rock-hard seat. *What am I gonna do for a job? Been working for Knickerbocker for a long time. What the hell am I thinking? Won't be so hard— ain't nothing so special about cleaning, painting, polishing, and shining.* He laughed as he remembered his king and prince of shine joke.

Nelson came back. "When I finished sweeping the floors outside the TB ward, I saw a young Black man all by himself away in the corner—either means he's real sick and they protecting the others or he's the healthiest and they looking out for him. Not close enough to read the name on the chart and I don't like going inside, anyway. My daddy died from TB a few years ago. Do you want to come take a peek through the window?"

"Sure thing."

"Follow me."

Nelson chuckled as he realized his guest was tiptoeing. "What the hell you doing? You worried about waking people up?"

"Yeah, I am."

"Don't worry, they can't hear you through the glass. These folks suffer from typhus, real nasty stuff, and the people with tuberculosis are around the corner. Hold on, one of the doctors is here. Not sure if he'll like me bringing you around. Let me go ask him."

Duane looked for another chair, which were in short supply, and rested against the wall, holding his shirtsleeve to his mouth.

⊷⟩◉ ◉⟨⊶

"Doc, a fella came over on the last boat looking for a Black survivor from the *Slocum* and I told him none of the victims were Colored. Then I spotted this young man over here who matches the fella's description."

"Yes, one of the tugs in the area dragged him out of the water. They found him floating on his back, unconscious. Where is the visitor?"

"Shit, should have brought him with me. Sorry, didn't mean to cuss."

⊷⟩◉ ◉⟨⊶

The doctor walked toward the patient and motioned for the two men to enter when they appeared in the doorway, but held up his hand in a signal to stop. He pointed to the masks on the wall. Both Nelson and Duane held the protective covering to their faces as they walked toward the bed.

Duane noticed all of the cuts on the legs and the scratches on the arms, and when the doctor stepped off to the side, he cried, "That's him! Is he okay?"

The doctor answered, "Not much physical damage other than these lacerations and bruises. He's also breathing well, so we assume he went into shock and his body needs time to recover. The men who fished him out of the river witnessed what he did—said he singlehandedly saved ten people, one at a time."

"Wow, Bodee's a hero!"

"I can only tell you what they told me, but it seems so. I didn't want to send an unconscious Black man to the mainland, especially a hero, expecting he'd receive the kind of treatment he deserves. The only problems here are the other patients—don't want him to contract anything before he comes to."

Nelson brought Duane his chair from the lobby and he settled in next to his friend. A few minutes later, the doctor returned with another mask. "You appear to be a little nervous about catching something. Relax, all the people in here are almost ready to go home and I got you by the window. I bet you he wakes up before the morning. Goodnight."

"How did the king and prince of shine get themselves into this mess, Mr. Rivers?" He glanced down halfheartedly hoping for a response and saw something unusual. "Boy, are you full of surprises." He removed an oddly shaped pepper shaker from his coworker's grip and then heard the whisper, "Where are we, Duane?"

Part Four

The Aftermath

CHAPTER 48

Homecoming

"Okay, Bodee. Take your time. The doc said your legs and arms might keep cramping up for a while. Let's wait under the tree for the afternoon ferry; sorry you were too weak to leave in the morning. You'll be home for dinner."

"Yeah, I feel better, but let's sit. Good idea, Duane, I'm still a little tired."

The crew of the small transport secured a line to the dock and exchanged some words with the doctor, who came down for Bodee's departure.

"Bodee, it was my honor to treat you. You are a true hero in every way. Your friend told me you don't want to say too much about what you did, but I heard firsthand, and you're the definition of courage and bravery. I did take the liberty of letting the captain here understand what you did. Take care of yourself."

"Thanks for all your help. I feel good today. Ready to go home."

"Take it easy for a few days and eat some of your favorite foods. Maybe fatten up a bit! You deserve some rest. Oh, and, Duane, no need to worry anymore about catching something—it really is okay to take at least one of those masks off now."

"Sure thing."

The men laughed and began to make their way to the back of the boat. "No, not the back," the captain said. "Heroes and their friends sit next to the captain. Right here, fellas. The doctor told me who you are, but I already heard about you. All of the operators around these waters talk. Lots of people saw what you did and we know better than anyone what it's like when you been in the water so long. You pushed through exhaustion so many times and never rested, and look at you, all skin and bones—don't understand how you found the strength. A few of us jumped in to help, but the fighting and the grabbing drains a swimmer like nothing else we ever seen. You're one amazing man and it will be my pleasure to bring you back to the mainland. Hang on."

The rocking of the ship and being in the water again triggered memories of twisted bodies, scratching and kicking, but then Bodee recalled the relief of coming to the surface with yet another survivor. He'd come so far with his ability to direct both his thoughts and his visions. The faces of the survivors would be his lasting images. *Yes, this what I'll hold onto.*

The ferry docked on the Bronx side and Bodee steadied his legs, leaning on his friend for support as he saw the steps to the elevated train in the far distance. He prepared himself for the long walk. The captain held his hand up for them to stop and pointed to a White man standing next to an automobile about twenty feet from where they stood. The man waved them over.

"You must be Bodee and Duane. My brother was the doctor at Riverside and he asked me to meet you. You're going to ride back home in style. Hop in—heroes in the front and friends in the back. Okay?"

"Sounds fine to us!" Bodee said.

"Call me Harry. Where to?"

"Minetta Lane."

"Where?"

"I'll show you. Head downtown."

"Whatever you say, Mr. Rivers."

⟶▬◉ ◉▬⟵

Bodee paused at the top of Minetta and peered down the block. Two short, but eventful, weeks earlier, he had taken his first tenuous walk down the lane worried about the criminals in the shadows. His former fear of danger and certain defeat was replaced by a new sense of belonging and triumph.

Juba, Nellie, and Marcus saw his approach from the window of the apartment, but they didn't run up to greet him because they wouldn't deprive him of his victory walk. All the locals—criminals, residents, even a few of the Whyos—gave him nods of respect as he made slow progress down the half block to his home. The story would never hit the news and no newsie would ever cry, "Extra!

Extra! Read about the hero of the *Slocum* disaster!" but those who mattered most to him were already informed and told to keep it quiet. The Knickerbocker Steamship Company would never hear his heroic tale because there was no better place in the world to keep a secret than on Minetta Lane.

Bodee shook Silvy's hand and received a "top of the evening," from Shamus McTiernan. Nellie couldn't hold back any longer and rushed to his side. She offered a tender kiss and a shoulder to lean on—exactly what she hoped to provide for years to come.

Juba and Marcus provided hugs, along with a picture taken by the photographer working the St. Mark's picnic. Bodee studied Helmut's face and tears began to flow, but Eddie's image holding his first hot dog brought on a broad smile. Juba whispered, "A lady by the name of Gerda Heinrich dropped this off and said these people were special to you. Also said you saved her little Eddie."

Bodee traced his fingers around the edges of the photograph and his grandmother anticipated his questions. "The mother and child are fine, but your friend Helmut didn't make it." A single tear streamed down Bodee's right cheek for his dear friend, and then a stream followed for the hundreds who perished. Juba touched the spot between his eyes, and he remembered the ten people he rescued. A feeling of satisfaction swept over him. Gone were the thoughts of *could I have done more*. Bodee held his girl by the waist and his grandma by the hand as Uncle Marcus led the way—the family headed upstairs for a proper celebration. Bodua, the protector, was home.

CHAPTER 49

June 15, 1905

THE CARNAGE OF the *General Slocum* was the deadliest disaster in the history of the United States. One thousand and thirty of the thirteen hundred passengers perished in the blaze, and the remains of sixty-one victims could not be identified. Fault for the tragedy was generally attributed to three parties: inspector Henry Lundberg, who evaluated the fire safety systems as being in working order; Frank Barnaby and the other executives of the Knickerbocker Steamship Company, who failed to invest in proper equipment and sought to cover up this fact; and Captain Van Schaik, who accepted the fraudulent inspections and never tested the gear or ran fire drills. In addition, the captain made the fatal decision to run into the wind toward North Brother Island, which fed the fire.

The inspector was prosecuted three times and mistrials were declared on each occasion. Prosecution of the Knickerbocker management depended on a successful action against Lundberg. Without this conviction, the courts had no choice but to accept Knickerbocker's claim that they relied on the passing inspections and assumed their crew adhered to company policies regarding testing the equipment and conducting fire drills. The captain, the only party convicted of wrongdoing, remained free while appealing his guilty verdict. Van Schaik began his ten-year sentence at Sing Sing in 1908—he was paroled three years later.

Virtually all of the deceased were interred in the Lutheran All Saints Cemetery in Middle Village, Queens. On the first anniversary of the fire, more than fifteen thousand people participated in a ceremony for the dedication of a twenty-foot statue commemorating the unidentified victims, all of whom were buried in a mass grave, later marked by the monument.

Newlyweds Bodee and Nellie Rivers, who had married a month earlier, found a spot to view the proceedings from a distance. The stares preceded the pointing and then the whispers began. After a few minutes, a group of five men walked toward the couple, who prepared to make a hasty departure.

Bodee whispered to his wife, "This happened to me once before when I went to the St. Mark's picnic. Seems like they're planning to ask us to go."

The couple turned to leave and the men called out, "Wait!"

"We not causing any trouble," Bodee shouted. "Only here to pay our respects is all. You don't want us here, no problem . . . we going."

The first man moved closer and smiled. "No. You misunderstand—you, you saved my wife."

Each man took their turn.

"And my little girl."

"My son."

"My niece."

The last man extended his hand. "You rescued me. Please join us."

The Rivers walked toward the grandstand with their escort and received a round of applause. Many of the people Bodee saved walked up and expressed their thanks. One gave them a commemorative pin which read, "We Mourn Our Loss." Another provided a section of black ribbon and fastened it to their sleeves. A woman noticed Nellie perspiring from the hot sun and offered her handkerchief.

Adella Liebenow, a young girl badly burned in the fire, pulled a long rope toward her, which removed the large American flag covering the structure. The crowd applauded as they admired the fourteen-foot granite foundation, which held four impressive statues—the two in the center measured six feet in height and those on the ends were half as tall. One of the larger images symbolized *faith* and depicted a man pointing to the heavens while staring intently at the other tall figure depicting *courage*—two sentiments in abundant supply on that fateful day. The two end statues represented *grief* and *despair*, which seemed fitting one year later.

The program began with the mournful sound of Chopin's "Funeral March" and children placed flowers around the base of the monument, including a wreath made of sixty-one roses, one for each of the unidentified dead. Opening prayers were delivered by Bishop Henry C. Potter of the Episcopal Church—Reverend Haas was conspicuously absent. After several speeches and musical interludes, the observance came to a close.

The Rivers said their goodbyes and, as they turned to leave, Gerda Heinrich and her two boys, Eddie and Tommy, approached from behind.

Eddie flashed one of his signature smiles. "Remember me?" He ducked and attached himself to Bodee's right leg, but quickly moved up and wrapped his arms around his savior's waist. Gerda walked toward Bodee's available arm and crawled under its protection.

Tommy displayed his smile, which now featured several more teeth, and introduced himself. "My name is Tommy and you never met me, but boy did I hear about you! None of us would be here together without what you did, but I'm not gonna do any of this hugging stuff, if that's okay."

"Fine with me."

Gerda opened her left arm and Tommy reconsidered as he found a comfortable place in her embrace. "I'm so sorry we haven't been in touch and I wasn't sure if it would be all right if we visited, but I did drop off the photograph from the picnic," she said. "Helmut's father gave it to me for Eddie and I thought your family would like to see the faces of some of the people you saved."

Bodee reached into his pocket and pulled out his copy of the photo. Gerda did the same. Eddie pointed. "Big day for me . . . my very first hot dog!"

Soon after the one-year anniversary, Bodee realized his dream and became a prominent baseball player in the Negro Leagues and lived in many cities around the country. He eventually settled back in New York after retiring from the sport. He never saw Gerda or Eddie again.

Within a year or two of the *Slocum* fire, Little Germany ceased to exist as the final wave of migration to other German neighborhoods like Yorkville took place. People who lost family members couldn't bear to stay—memories were everywhere.

The memorials were well attended for many years and mentions of the tragedy continued to occupy numerous pages in the local papers as the criminal prosecutions took their course. In time, the number of people attending the annual remembrance dwindled—focus turned to new disasters like the Triangle Shirtwaist Factory Fire in 1911, which took the lives of a hundred and forty-six garment workers, and the sinking of the *Titanic*, which claimed more than fifteen hundred. After World War I, and then again after World War II, the numbers were negligible as celebrations of all things German became politically incorrect. Some families, however, chose to remember the events of June 15, 1904, and small groups still paid their respects every year.

CHAPTER 50

June 15, 2017

CHRISTIAN RIVERS, A longtime professor at Monroe College in the Bronx, made his annual trek to the monument in Queens. According to stories handed down over the years, his great-grandfather Bodee had been a crew member on the *Slocum* and courageously rescued many during the aftermath of the fire. The professor spent years documenting his family history and could trace his roots all the way back to the Ashanti in Africa in the late 1700s. He was never able to document his ancestor's employment on the ship, however, as all of the records of those working that day omitted his name. Still, the Rivers family made their regular excursion to the cemetery every June when he was a child and he chose to continue this tradition.

Young Christian Rivers found the tales of his great-grandfather fascinating—hero and star baseball player, as brave as they come and fast as the wind. A more mature Christian hoped at least one of his two high school age boys would become similarly interested, so the annual visits to the Lutheran All Saints Cemetery would continue for another generation.

He walked to the granite base of the statue and read the inscription out loud: *Erected by the Organization of General Survivors and the Public, in the Memory of the 61 Unidentified Dead Who Lost Their Lives on the Steamboat Gen. Slocum on June 15, 1904.* He paused for a moment before he read the final two words, "In Memoriam," and turned when he heard the same phrase echoed from behind.

"Oh, hi," he said.

"Seemed like you needed a little help finishing up."

He glanced at the exotic woman before him with hints of White, Black, and Asian all rolled up into one beautiful package. She extended her hand and he noticed an elegant design on her right forearm. Christian never liked tattoos much, but hers accentuated what was already so attractive. *A leaf? No, a symbol of some kind. I wish I could take a better look.*

He realized he had left his new acquaintance hanging and after they shook hands, she smiled, and his knees slightly buckled. "Are you okay?" she laughed. "They always told me about my million-dollar smile, but I never made anyone fall to the ground!"

He regrouped. "Sorry, my mind wandered—my name is Christian."

"I'm Wilhelmina, and I know my name, which is classic German, doesn't fit the face. I've got a little bit of everything in me. Think of me as a cocktail." She twirled as she shuffled from side to side and he thought, *How does this movement in any way relate to a cocktail? Doesn't matter, I could watch her do that all day!*

"A tasty one to be sure!" he said, causing his inner voice to kick in. *How stupid was that remark! Go slow, dial everything back—you've replayed this scene in your dreams for years. You knew this would happen, just like they all do. She's the one. Don't screw this up!* "So sorry, miss, I didn't mean to be so forward. Maybe it *was* your smile that got the better of me."

"Okay, no offense taken, and thanks for the compliment."

Christian took a deep breath in order to calm down and make sure this moment would play out well. He had never dated seriously since his wife passed away ten years ago, and always wished the woman from his recurring vision would be the one. *This is my chance, don't blow it.*

He offered, "They say my great-grandfather worked on the ship and survived the terrible fire."

"I guessed he did; otherwise, this conversation might be difficult."

"Oh yeah, right!"

"My grandpa was one of the surviving children on the boat."

"The experience must have scarred him for life."

"Actually, no. He always said June 15, 1904, made him into who he was and taught him about courage."

"Courage?"

"Yes, but not only his own. He spoke a lot about that day and those who sacrificed so much to save others. I can show you one of the heroes, if you like?"

"Sure."

"Take a peek at this photo taken a few days before the fire." She reached into her purse and pulled out her phone. "I created a digital image of the old photograph many years ago—the original is on its last legs."

She walked next to him and leaned in as she scrolled through her photos and he spotted another tiny tattoo on the back of her neck beneath her hairline. *Another symbol of some kind. Beautiful, just like her.* Her neck-length black hair picked up a breeze and blew into his face—he savored the scent. *Lilacs,* he thought.

"Christian, I keep losing you . . . over here." She snapped her fingers and held up her phone "Are you a daydreamer or something? My Grandpa Eddie is the cute little boy."

Most of his visions included a surprise—something he didn't foresee or misinterpreted—often these twists were unwelcome, but he never saw this coming. Christian didn't respond, but reached into his wallet and handed her a laminated photograph he kept on a small card.

"It can't be," she said. "How did you get my photo? What's going on here?"

"Hold on—I consider this to be my picture as well—handed down over the years. The original, I guess like yours, is old and delicate. This is the one I bring with me when I come to the memorial. I never understood how my great-grandfather Bodee could have been friends with these other people, given the year and his color compared to theirs."

She stared at him. "Your great-grandfather is the Black man in this picture? The hero? What's your last name?"

"Rivers."

"My God. How can this be? You are Bodee Rivers's great-grandchild and I am Eddie Heinrich's granddaughter. What are the chances of the two of us meeting like this?"

He couldn't respond honestly—they were destined to meet. She was the woman from his dream, but he had no idea of the connection of their ancestors. He told some friends about his visions from time to time, but they often considered this to be crazy talk, so he stopped trying to explain—he was not about to start again now. His unusual family ability often skipped generations, but his father had it and his granddad did not. Christian was unsure, however, about his great-grandfather.

"This is so amazing. Your great-grandfather was a Black man, and look at you, you're . . ."

"Careful, Wilhelmina! Your grandpa couldn't have been more White and you're . . ."

They both laughed and Wilhelmina gave him a hug, taking hold of both of his hands. She whispered, "I guess you're a cocktail too!" She stepped closer for another embrace and he didn't want to let go.

Their moment was disturbed by a beautiful red bird that landed on top of the part of the statue symbolizing *faith*. The creature looked to the sky and the couple admired the black feathers surrounding its eyes, which gave the appearance of a mask. Another red bird appeared in the distance and swooped in, making a dramatic dive toward its friend. It slowed as it approached and settled on top of the other tall statue representing *courage*.

Wilhelmina studied their two majestic visitors. One had its attention trained on her and the other on Christian. "I think we should get out of here before this gets any weirder," she said. He chuckled but agreed, and they started to walk toward the street.

She pointed. "Christian, over there, outside the gate—see it? A hot dog stand! Grandpa Eddie always used to say there's nothing better in the world than a New York hot dog!"

"Your grandfather was a smart man. My treat."

Historical Notes & Liberties

Part I: New York, 1904

The book takes place during the period immediately following the creation of New York City as we know it today. In the 1890s, Chicago began to redefine itself with an expanded footprint, and New York became worried about its claim to being the largest in the country. The consolidation vote in Brooklyn was very close and passed by a margin of just 277 votes. Brooklyn experienced a tough transitional period as it went from being the third-largest city in the country to a mere borough. The consolidation became effective in 1898 and grouped Manhattan, the Bronx, Staten Island, and Western Queens into one municipality. The three towns of Eastern Queens became suburban Nassau County.

Much of the first section of the book takes place on Minetta Lane. The depiction of this part of Manhattan, which was given the nickname of the Bend, was accurate except for the time period. My description was spot-on for the early 1890s. During Theodore Roosevelt's time as police commissioner in New York City (1895–1897), the Bend started to become a safer part of New York. By 1904, it was not the notorious neighborhood described in these pages.

The Bend was a home for Blacks around the time that slavery ended in New York (1827). Initially, it was referred to as "Little Africa" and the path the residents built along a narrow stream, which ran through the area, was called the "Negroe's Causeway." Once the stream was boarded over and a proper road built on top, the Causeway became Minetta Street. All of the residents of the Bend were fictional, although two of them, Juba and Blood, were inspired by characters in Stephen Crane's short story "Minetta Lane, New York."

The background about the newsies was also accurate, including the description of the routine in the Newsboys Lodging House, which was a real facility on the corner of Duane and Chambers Streets. During those years, many young boys lived on the street and worked as newsies, assuming colorful nicknames. The description of Newspaper Row was also accurate.

Kleindeutschland, or Little Germany, was accurately depicted in the book. By 1904, it was on the decline as many families had already moved uptown to Yorkville. This part of the city was bounded by Avenue D on the West, the Bowery to the East, Fourteenth Street to the north, and Division Street to the south. Avenue B, which was the commercial heart of the community, was also called German Broadway. At the peak of its popularity in the late 1800s, Little Germany was the home to the third-largest population of Germans anywhere in the world.

The sections relating to the St. Mark's Evangelical Lutheran Church were historically accurate except for the picnic the Saturday before the excursion, which did not take place.

The section of the novel that described floating baths was historically accurate and my description was based on an actual bath in use around that time. The floating baths provided a means through which city residents could find some relief from the heat during this period, which preceded air-conditioning and fans.

The Draft Riots of 1863, which pitted the Irish against the Blacks and the rich, are briefly mentioned in Part One. Blacks were targeted because the Irish were infuriated at the prospect of being drafted to fight in a war that would free the people (Blacks) who would likely steal their jobs. Blacks were beaten severely and a number were lynched by roving Irish mobs. Many homes of the rich were ransacked and some wealthy New Yorkers were physically attacked because the Irish were incensed they were able to pay a fee to be exempted from the draft.

Weeksville, a small section of Brooklyn that was dominated by free Black landowners before the Civil War, is mentioned in the book. It was located where Crown Heights stands today. By 1904, the area was quite mixed, but some of the old institutions, like Colored School No. 2 and the Berean Baptist Church, were still in existence.

The Whyos were an actual gang that existed around this period. As with the Bend, I took some liberties with dates. This gang was already defunct by 1904. My depiction of their activities and strength would have been accurate for the 1880s or early 1890s. They did, in fact, have the curious musical signals I described in the book and they also socialized in the black-and-tan saloons in the Bend, upon which the bar "Snake Eyes" was based.

Most of the other characters in Part One were fictional except for Reverend George Haas and the captain of the *SS Grand Republic*, John Pease. The Knickerbocker Steamship Company was the owner of the *SS Grand Republic*, and Frank Barnaby was the president of the company.

Part II: The Dream

Most of the characters introduced or developed in this section were fictional except for Mayor George McClellan, the son of the famous Civil War general of the same name. He was one of the youngest mayors in New York City and he did have presidential aspirations. McClellan ran in 1904 and received three votes at the Democratic National Convention. The mayor attended the Schuetzen Bund Parade in 1904 as described in the novel.

The Gerda Heinrich character was fictional, but inspired by the actual organizer of the 17th Annual St. Mark's Annual Excursion, Mary Abendschein, an unmarried woman in her thirties.

The references to baseball teams were historically accurate. The New York Highlanders played at Hilltop Stadium, on the west side of Broadway between 165th and 168th Streets. This team became the New York Yankees in 1913. The Brooklyn Monitors were an actual baseball team in the Negro Leagues.

Part III: June 15, 1904

All of the details about the *General Slocum* are generally historically accurate. I used the actual crew names in the novel, with the exception of the main character, Bodee Rivers, who was fictional. The Maurer and Haas families were actual passengers on the *General Slocum*. The ships that came to the rescue of the passengers, *John Wade*, *Massasoit*, and *Zophar Mills*, performed as described in the book. The heroic exploits of Bodee Rivers were inspired by the actions of Carl

Rappaport, the coxswain of the *Massasoit*, who singlehandedly pulled several victims to the safety of his boat. The details regarding the spread of the fire on the ship are also accurate, and my description about how the fire started was similar to one of the commonly accepted theories.

Part IV: The Aftermath
The facts given about the number of deaths and the criminal prosecutions were all accurate, as was the description of the monument in the Lutheran All Saints Cemetery. It is interesting to note that while most of the literature regarding the fire lists the date as June 15, some sources, including the inscription on this monument, list it as June 14.

The final two characters introduced in the novel, Christian Rivers and Wilhelmina Heinrich, were fictional.

Acknowledgements & Sources

I used the following sources during the research phase of my novel: *Empire City: New York Through the Centuries*, Kenneth T. Jackson and David S. Dunbar, Editors; *Ship Ablaze: The Tragedy of the Steamboat General Slocum*, Edward T. O'Donnell; *German New York City*, Richard Panchyk; "Minetta Lane, New York," Stephen Crane; *By a Margin of 277 Votes: The Consolidation of Brooklyn and New York*, Long Island Historical Journal, Donald E. Simon; *Strange and Obscure Stories of New York City*, Tim Rowland.

About the Author

A. Robert Allen has published four novels and two short-story prequels in his *Slavery and Beyond* series. All are stand-alone stories connected by theme. He writes historical fiction that transports readers to times and places immediately before or soon after the end of slavery. A. Robert is a long-time higher education professional and resides in New York. The first volume in the series, *Failed Moments*, is a fictional account of Allen's ancestors in 1790 during the slave revolution in what would become Haiti and later in 1863 during New York's Draft Riots. The second volume, *A Wave From Mama*, immerses readers in racially charged post Civil War Brooklyn and gives an interesting look at the building of the Brooklyn Bridge. The third book in the series, *Minetta Lane*, takes place in 1904 in a downtown New York neighborhood that lives by an unusual race-based code. The prequel to this third volume, Minetta Mornings, takes place twenty-five years earlier. His most recent release, Living in the Middle, transports readers to perhaps the most violent and significant incident of racial violence in U.S. history, the Tulsa Race Riots of 1921. The prequel to this novel, which takes place in 1896, is entitled Ticket to Tulsa. Find out more about the author and his works at his website: http://arobertallen.com

Get Exclusive Materials

I find the best thing about writing to be the fun associated with creating characters and my favorite part of publishing is the relationships I develop with readers. Given my trouble saying goodbye to my characters, I write prequels and sequels for my books and provide this content exclusively for the readers on my mailing list. Go to http://arobertallen.com to join and pick up all of this free additional content, which includes the prequel to Minetta Lane. This short story explains how Juba and Blood became established on the block twenty-five years earlier.

Also by A. Robert Allen

Failed Moments

A Wave From Mama

Living in the Middle

Minetta Mornings (Prequel to Minetta Lane)

Ticket to Tulsa (Prequel to Living in the Middle)